Catcher's Keeper

a novel

by JD Spero

"The thing is, it drives me crazy if somebody gets killed—especially somebody very smart and entertaining and all—and it's somebody else's fault."
– Holden Caulfield
(on the death of Mercutio in Romeo and Juliet*)*

**Contact author for book club bookings or
school visits at:**
www.jdspero.com
https://www.facebook.com/jdspero
@jdspero

Catcher's Keeper copyright ©2014 by JD Spero
ISBN: 978-1495992780

Cover photo courtesy of Prillfoto & Dreamstime.com
Cover by Joleene Naylor
Printed by CreateSpace

Catcher's Keeper

a novel

by JD Spero

TABLE OF CONTENTS

Chapter 1
Alden

Not even a week since I moved in with my brother and he's testing my pacifist nature, butting in on my shit.

The aroma of coffee leads me like Pepé Le Pew to Penelope—right to Jerry. He's at the kitchen table, all showered and dressed in Polo, going through my file box like he's researching at the goddam library. He could at least *pretend* he's helping me unpack. He's into my old black binder from school. The thing must be decades old. Why can't he wait until I'm out of the house to go through my shit like a normal nosy brother? It's a Catch-22, though, because if I tell him to stop, he'll know I'm buggin' out. Can't give him that.

Besides, he's allowing my forty-year-old ass to crash here and I have yet to ask my big favor. So I should probably let this slide.

The coffee maker just made its final, steamy percolation. Pavlov's so right.

I like my coffee black. Jerry has a hodgepodge collection of mugs. Surprising since he'd been married so long. You'd think he'd have matching china and whatnot. But no, I pour my joe into a YMCA mug and check out his lame view. What I'd call "low LA." Parking lot. Smoke-stacks. Bird shit. Litter. The view is so pitiful I almost forgive Jerry for snooping. But then he reads aloud from my black binder, which is still in his hands:

"*Now he's out in Hollywood being a prostitute. If there's one thing I hate, it's the movies. Don't even mention them to me.*"

It's familiar, but far away. There's this tingling behind my eyes—like that time the fuzz found a doobie in my shirt pocket. I'm caught. Ol' YMCA feels heavy as I take my first sip. It's hot and tangy and gets my stomach ready. But I can't find my smokes anywhere.

"Jesus, Alden," Jerry says. "What *is* this?"

It's quiet but for pages turning. Maybe it's the coffee, but I start to sweat.

"You seen my cigarettes?"

Jerry just keeps reading. He's all hunched over, rubbing his bald spot. It comes to me all at once, what he's reading: my journal from when I was sixteen. That thing I wrote for the doc at the funny farm. Watching him read that is like having an itch out of reach.

My next sip of coffee is rushed and traces my esophagus with a nice burn. I would kill for a cigarette. I finally find my box of Marlboros behind the toaster. And it's empty.

"Don't you have any goddam smokes?"

Jerry takes his time answering, his eyes never leaving my binder. "Told you, I quit years ago."

"Doesn't Janine have some? I mean, did she? Maybe you stashed them away somewhere?"

That sure makes him look up. He glares at me. I feel bad, but it's the nicotine talking. When he opens his mouth, though, what he says is, "This is good, Alden. All this about Spencer and the *Atlantic Monthly* and the ducks. You've captured something here."

For real? This is my *journal* he's talking about. I'd rather him wear my goddam briefs than read that thing. Word. I gotta get some air, let myself out into the sunshine. It's like I'm taking up too much space in his pad. Him reading that thing is spreading the cells of my body all around the goddam room, my whole self pinging around, getting bruised, defenseless. Man, this place is gloomy as hell. The lame view is not half of it.

I drain ol' YMCA. Let him read it if he wants to. I'm going out to buy smokes. Maybe some eggs too. In the spare room, I pull on cutoffs and my favorite Dylan t-shirt with a tomato stain on ol' Dylan's face. Where the hell are my kicks? You'd think they'd jump out at you since Jerry's place is small compared to that stellar crib he had with Janine. Beyond small. Claustrophobic now that I have to wade through the cells of my own body to find my goddam shoes. Not the most Zen feeling in the world.

My Adidas finally appear under the coffee table. I'm putting them on my bare feet when Jerry says, "I knew you had balls, Alden. But not this big." He laughs, a snicker, as if he's uncovered my stash of *Playboy*s. "Not this big."

The last ounce drains out of me. I have to glance over to make sure he's really not looking at my *Playboy*s. No, still my goddam journal. So my options are this: I either have to rip it from his hands and confront him about it, or get the hell out of Dodge.

I'm a pacifist. And I still need that favor. So I'm out.

Slam the door. Probably should tell Jerry where I'm headed, but he's a smart dude. He'll figure it out.

Should've worn a jacket. Ol' Dylan can't do anything to keep me warm. The wind is hardcore. It'll warm up later. I mean, geez, it's September in LA.

Now that I have room to breathe, I can think. Maybe something's up with Jerry. Maybe that's why he's clinging to my journal. Last night at the Break Room, he just downed his brew and stared off at the boob tube across the bar. Maybe he was thinking about the ex? I dunno. He nodded as I gabbed on, but his timing was off. I mean, he *heard* me, but that was about it. So I never did get to ask him that favor—even though that had been the plan.

I need his help. See, I've written a novel and I want to publish it. And since Jerry's got all the contacts here in Hollywood...I mean, I wish I could tell you I came here to bond with my big bro, but it ain't so. I want to be an author, like, officially. Jerry can help me get an agent and get published because he's all connected in the industry. That's my plan, anyway.

My novel is about my other (younger) brother, Allie, who died from leukemia when he was eleven. I rebuilt his life in pages, filled in the blanks. It's heavy. I shot for non-fiction, tried to give the real deal. But he hadn't *lived* enough. So I had to make up some stuff. But I made his eleven years kick-ass, because he deserves that. I polished my prose to make it all literary and formal too. I can be very spiritual about Allie. He was, like, an old soul. He knew things. Like that time before he got sick, he knew what was up at my boarding school before I said a thing.

I'd had a bad time of it. Big surprise, right? I was the sleep-away kid, I get that. Even if Mom went to her grave regretting that decision, she and Dad sent me away. Them's the facts. So, this kid in my dorm, Randy Fletcher. What a cheese-weasel. Thought he was the bomb, though, talking static about all the brawls he'd get into with his *own cousin* in Jersey. Just a mean dude. He singled out this kid, Marty Horn. Horn had a funny look about him. All skin and bones, with these massive glasses. But harmless, stayed on the down-low. Kept to his books. Anyway. It started slow, like Fletch laying a gasser on his pillow, then it built up from there. Fletch called him names with acid on his tongue: Horny-Toad, Trombone, Bogart. Then it got physical. Once I walked into the can and Fletch was clutching Horn's arm, wringing his skin tighter than a tourniquet. Made me sick. But what'd I do? I asked Fletch if he wanted to catch a *movie* with me. It was lame. Word. I mean, it worked. Fletch let go and we split. But Horn was left crying. Made me feel like a real creep. Like I was in cahoots with Fletch. I wasn't, but Horn couldn't know that.

You're probably wondering what this had to do with Allie. Well, when I was home for Turkey break, the deal with Horn and Fletch irked me so much I lost sleep. Before I said word one, Allie said, "You know, Alden. You're out there at school far, far away. You all should take care of each other." Here he was, a nine-year-old boy, and he totally got it. I almost cried when he said that, but I grinned real big and told him, "Don't you worry about your big brother. No one's being mean to me."

And you know what he said back?

"You need to take care of others too, though."

Just like that. Word. This kid was something else. I listened too. I'd planned to go back and set Fletch straight, do whatever to stay in Horn's corner. But I never got the chance. Horn never came back after Turkey break. I still told Fletch what's what, but he didn't give a hoot by then.

Anyway, that's what my book is about. Allie and his, like, mystical intuition. Hurt like hell to write, days and weeks of hurt, but when I got it down, it felt good.

It was my little sister, Fiona—my favorite person in the world—who suggested I go to Jerry for help. Ol' Fiona is always coming up with those killer ideas. She's my number-one confidante. She's actually reading my manuscript—I called it *Allie*—right now.

The Mobil station on the corner glows in the dim California haze. The cashier, teenaged punk with black jelly bracelets up both arms, rings up my smokes, and doesn't say word one when I light up right there. That kills me. So does her fashion sense. I'm not cool with these new styles. The eighties are going to be cheesy, I can tell. I will always dig the seventies. Even the disco.

"You gotta phone here?" I ask.

"Outside. Around back," she says, pointing her thumb.

Groovy. No one will listen in on my confab with Fiona. Another pet peeve: a lot of phone booths in California have been truncated. Halfsies with no leg protection, no privacy. Why can't we be London-cool and have those bright red deals, like something from a cartoon?

Calculating West to East-coast time, Fiona is probably just finishing lunch. Sweet. I call her collect, as she made me promise to.

"Hi brother!" she says, all happy. She means it too.

It's awesome to hear her voice. I can just picture her: wrapped in a throw, curled on the couch, maybe some tea brewing nearby. "How's big Dave?"

She laughs. "Big Dave is fine. He's at work."

"I didn't wake you up from a nap or anything?" Her voice does sound a little scratchy.

"No. I actually…I was reading your manuscript, *Allie*."

"No way! For real?" My face goes all hot. The picture totally changes. She's not wrapped in a throw drinking tea; her hair is pulled back and she's at the kitchen table, pencil in hand, making dainty cursive comments in my binder.

"Yeah. About halfway done."

What does she think of it? I'm dying to know. But I don't ask. I'm a real pansy. "Oh, why don't I let you get back to it? If you're on a roll." Now *my* voice sounds scratchy and I wish I had bought a Coke. I stamp out my smoke.

"Oh, that's okay. I was just going to take a break anyway. Get something to drink."

Taking a break. Does that mean she doesn't like it? Her slippers swish across the kitchen tile, and I force a smile even though she can't see me. Someone told me that trick a while ago. Supposed to make your voice mellow. "Do I need to let you go so you can get a drink?" I say, that fake smile not working at all.

She laughs again. "No, sweetie."

My stomach twists when she says that. For the rest of our talk I can't stop thinking of Teresa. I'll fill you in on that later.

Her voice is all peppy now that she's whet her whistle. "So, how are things with Jerry? Are you all settled in? I would love to be a fly on the wall to see you two living together. Then again, maybe I wouldn't!" She gets a good chuckle out of that.

"It's cool. Good, I mean. Just got here. Last night we went out. Had some brews. Caught up."

"How's he doing? Did he mention Janine?"

That makes me feel like a dickweed, remembering what I said about her smokes. "Nah. He seems okay. I told him about my book but didn't ask him about the agent thing."

"Well, give it time. There's no deadline you're working with here."

"Right." It's killing me not knowing whether she digs my book. But now Teresa is in my way and there's no option but to get off the goddam line. "So, let's chat after you finish it, the whole manuscript. I'd totally love to hear what you think of it."

"Oh...okay."

Was that a pause? Does that mean she hates it?

I have to get off. Teresa is right there. It hurts.

"Okay, Fiona. Love ya, kid."

All those fluorescent lights in the Mobil station are depressing now that the sky has brightened up. But I'm parched. I buy a Coke and a sleeve of white-powdered doughnuts from Bracelets and decide to take a different route back to Jerry's. I'm not psyched about being there right now. I have that hitch in my stomach, the one I used to always get on my way to Dr. Santini's office, or to that last, unfortunate meeting with Mr. Spencer.

The neighborhood I'm walking through, smoking square after square, has an old baseball field. It's, like, smack in the middle of all these houses. There's no school next to it, just a baseball field. Barren. Empty. Weathered benches where dugouts should be, a big hole in the home plate fence. Doesn't look like it's hosted a game for a while. I walk right on by, flicking my butt into the batter's box like a punk. It's rude, I get it. I don't even know why I do it, honestly. It's not like it makes me feel any better.

Back at Jerry's, I can't believe my eyes. He's on the couch, his feet propped on the coffee table with my journal on his lap. He's *still* reading it?

My insides are going through the Mouli grater. Not cool. I gotta get him to stop reading or I'm going to ralph. I do that thing I used to do, toss up a silent prayer to my little brother: *Don't let me disappear, Allie. Don't let me disappear.*

But to Jerry, I act cool. That Catch-22 thing is still in effect. "Jerry, what's the buzz? Don't you have to get to work or something?" Geez, I sound like a whiny little girl.

"I'm a writer, Alden. I work from home."

Oh yeah. My fingertips are itching to grab the goddam thing from him. I try a different tack and offer him a doughnut. He takes it and keeps reading, white-powdered sugar sticking to his lips. Can't dude give it a break? Maybe coffee. I get him some with lots of cream. Jerry likes it on the light side. But he barely lifts his eyes when he takes the mug from me.

Finally, I stand right in front of him, and the cells of my body fly off the page he's reading and whack me in the chest. I snap, "So why are you reading that thing?"

He closes the binder and looks up at me. I'm relieved to the moon and can feel myself coming back. "Wow, Alden. You didn't actually write this when—"

"Yeah," I say, "after flunking out of Pencey." I play it cool.

"The shrink at the funny farm had me document my last few days…my rite of passage through New York City." My mouth tastes like I just had confession. I zip it and sit on the butterfly chair since he's sitting in the middle of the goddam couch.

He shakes his head, frowning down at the binder—my binder—in his hands.

I frown too. "Not my favorite memory, Jerry. I think the doc thought it would help. Catharsis."

"Did it?" Jerry asks. His face kills me, all concerned.

"Sure, it helped. Convinced me to quit organized education and pursue writing. Look at me now, brotha. I'm totally successful." My sarcasm falls flat. A trust fund kid is all I am, and he knows it. But that's not what he's getting at. The sun's pounding in and the place is heating up. I close the blinds, but as soon as I do, Jerry clicks on the lamp.

He cradles the binder in his hands. "And the voice. It's amazing."

I bark out a laugh. "Jerry! I was sixteen."

"Alden, I know. That's the beauty of it. It's so pure."

"You're a real comedian, you know that?"

Enough of this. He's not going to give my binder up, and I can't stand watching him not do it. What I need is a distraction. I know! I'll get my manuscript *Allie* and mark it up a little. The editing process is never done, they say. I leave Jerry on the couch and go to the spare room.

I hear Jerry call, "You could publish this, you know."

My jaw drops on that one. He said the magic "p" word, but it's all wrong. This isn't how it's supposed to go.

"That's not gonna happen," I say, but I doubt he hears me.

My manuscript *Allie* is in this clean white binder at the bottom of my suitcase. I love the weight of it. Substantial. I'm jonesing to work on it again. *This* is what I want to publish: *Allie*. Now, a pencil. I don't like editing in pen because I change my mind all the time. No pencils in any of Jerry's desk drawers. All these ripped envelopes and slips of paper and about a zillion red pens. But not one pencil. I don't want to go back out there, but I do.

"Yo Jerr, where do you keep your pencils?"

He's back at it, reading from my binder again. He's scrunching his forehead, all serious. In the next second he busts a gut. My fists clench instinctively, but I'm a pacifist. I shake them out and hit the kitchen in search of a pencil.

I get a little pang for Mom as I rifle through the drawer by the fridge. She always had a junk drawer where I would find pencils as a kid. Funny how little things like this remind me of her. Makes me sad to think she won't be able to read *Allie*. But it's good that Allie's got Mom with him now. He was all by himself for so long. It's nice to think of them together.

All I find is one of those short deals, like from a golf course. It reminds me of the club, how we'd go there as kids for Sunday brunch all dressed up like Christmas ornaments. We'd have to act all civilized, but I could always get Allie laughing at a good clip. Good ol' red-faced, shoulder-shake laughing that burst out like a balloon popping. Never fail, oatmeal or something would fly out of his nose. Ha! That gives me an idea! Now I'm dying for a pencil. My hands start to get sweaty over it.

"Jerry, can you get me a goddam pencil?"

He's off the couch, stretching his arms all over the place, my journal left behind on the cushions. Finally!

"What do you think this is, Alden, kindergarten? I don't have pencils."

He goes to the can.

"What the hell do you use to make edits, then?" I call to him as he's peeing. It's not a completely rhetorical question. I mean, Jerry is the experienced writer. It is possible I could learn a thing or two.

He flushes and goes to his room. "The red pen," he says, coming towards me with a sinister smile, and hands it over.

I get to work right there at the kitchen table, hoping to shake all those lovely teenaged memories Jerry so kindly dredged up. Okay. Now...where to add the scene about Allie's oatmeal coming out of his nose? I fan the pages, speed read.

Jerry sits across from me. "I have a word processor in the spare room. Why don't you use that?"

He's got a point. My handwriting is butt-ugly. Total chicken scratch. Back when I traveled to San Diego with my posse we kinda boycotted machines. Convenience was the enemy. Seems bogus now, but we wanted to bond with nature—and typewriters didn't fit in the scene. That's why I like pencils. You can feel the tree in it. Smell the wood. But I'm over it now. For one thing, it's a pain to write by hand. I've got this terrific callus on my middle finger. Looks like a big, flat wart. I wrote the whole thing out, photocopied it for Fiona, and punched it into this white binder. But if it were typed, like, in print? It would look like a real book. Allie would love it. I must smile, because Jerry taps my shoulder all chummy.

"I can go to my agent's office," he says. "They have space I can use. And a machine. I can work there."

He brings me into the spare room. My junk is strewn all over but Jerry doesn't seem to care. He turns on his word processor and explains how to work it. It's totally gravy. Like a typewriter, except you can change stuff, edit on the spot. That's another thing I never liked about typewriters: permanent mistakes. But here, you can erase. Like it never happened. How could I have shunned such stellar conveniences?

"I'm serious about your journal, Alden. I think you could publish it. You know, as a memoir."

Okay, now I'm losing my cool. "Jerry! What the—? Jump back, all right? You're telling me to publish my teenage *depression*, do you get it? You're asking me to print—like, immortalize—the lowest point of my life. You are so outta line."

Jerry squeezes my shoulder, unfazed. "Well, who knows?" he says. "Maybe this would make it a positive thing. You've got something there. It's funny. And touching."

Dude is not getting it. My adolescent cells are whapping me in the face like I'm sitting in a goddam hailstorm. Breathe. *Don't let me disappear...*

"Fuck you, Jerry."

Gotta keep busy. Distraction. I start typing with Jerry still standing there. He can stay or go; I don't care. I chill out as I type. I get three paragraphs down when I hear him check out. The door is one of those heavy deals that slams shut even when you don't mean it to. Shakes the whole place. My signal to take a goddam break. I feel like I've been run over. I need to veg out. Get some orange juice or something.

I flip on the boob tube, just to see. Jerry has a very high-end television and I get sucked in to this game show. I slide onto the couch with my orange juice and prop my feet on the coffee table like Jerry did. Comfy. I'm kinda watching and not watching Chuck Woolery.

Why do I still feel so edgy? Jerry was so engrossed in that journal. I don't know why he wants to read it. I don't know why *anyone* would want to read it. And he thinks it could be published? I have a knot in my stomach over it. Maybe I should go out for some air. This place is suffocating.

I click off the tube. Jerry has left the lamp on, so I click that off too. But then something is missing. I sat right on the couch and didn't notice? I put the lamp back on, even though I don't need it to see. I even open the blinds, as if the sun's rays could give me the lowdown. I'm bugging out. Jerry has taken it. My journal is gone.

Chapter 2
Jerry

I have Alden's black binder propped between me and the steering wheel outside Mitch's office, letting it sink in. I'm hugging the thing to my chest, knowing what's coming, but hoping it doesn't. Of course, it does. When the tears come, they come in droves. I'm glad I stayed in the car.

Damn, that was a long time ago. Nearly twenty-five years. Since I was the only one who lived near the clinic, I was expected to visit him on a regular basis. I went in once to surprise him. (Bad idea, by the way. Surprise visits to a psychiatric ward are never a good idea.) He was sitting in this hard chair staring at what I thought was a window but turned out to be a piece of art. And I hate to say this because I am an artist myself, but it was *bad* art. Alden had a look on his face I'd never seen before. Scared. I know it wasn't the bad art that scared him, but the juxtaposition was unnerving. It's funny: I spoke with a handful of nurses who all gave me the same line about Alden's condition, but seeing him stare at that bad art with that look on his face? That's what convinced me that my little brother needed help. I left the ward without visiting him that day. Turned right around. I went again the day after, but you bet I called first.

That's when things got weirder. After I called, I went in to see him, and he was sitting in the rec room near the ping-pong table. I got right to it, picked up a paddle and invited him to play. I never intended to be a therapist for him, just a familiar face. He obliged me and grabbed a paddle. But after a few volleys he smacked that little white ball with such force it nearly put a dent in the wall. It missed my ear by just a few inches.

"What the hell was that?" I said.

Alden was so red in the face, I could practically see steam shooting from his ears.

"What's up, Alden? What's wrong?"

He fell back onto the sofa, his arms crossed. "Why are you here, Jerry?"

"What do you mean? I'm here to visit you."

"To visit me? Really?" His face was all twisted like he was about to cry.

"Listen, I don't want to upset you or anything," I said, tossing the paddle on the table. "If you want me to leave—"

"Yeah. I think you should leave."

I told myself not to take it personally. "Okay. I'll come back tomorrow."

"Nah," Alden said. He sniffed hard like he was holding in tears.

This may have been a mistake, but I sat next to him on the sofa. "Alden, are you okay? Did something happen?"

He laughed then, but it was stiff, forced. "Did something happen?" he mocked. "Yes, Jerry. I guess something must have happened for me to land in the funny farm."

"Come on, Alden. It's just a temporary thing." I put my arm around him. Or tried to. He shoved me away and stood up.

"Just go away." He was definitely crying now. "Please."

It wasn't until a few days later when I was denied entrance that I realized Alden had been serious when he said he didn't want me to come back. A robust lady in scrubs set her fists on her hips at the front desk. "Under no circumstances. Can't come in. Patients have rights too."

She had to be joking. "He's my brother."

"Don't matter. He don't want you comin' around no more."

I stared at her, this stranger telling me I was no longer allowed to visit my own brother. It didn't make sense. There had to have been a mistake. But when I tried again the next day and a different nurse relayed the same message, it was like someone reached inside me and pulled out everything I had. I was hollow.

Shit. All these years—I realize now—I've been pissed about that. Incredulous Alden would reject his own brother—the only one in our family who was actually *there* for him. Which is why I was so shocked when he called a few months ago to suggest we shack up together.

"Why don't you ask Dad?" I said, knee-jerk. He'd have plenty of room, the bastard.

Alden just chuckled. "Afraid I used up all my quarters on that one, brotha."

While he used a video game analogy to excuse his non-relationship with our father, he made moving in with me sound like a TV show—two middle-aged bachelor brothers (with zilch in common, I might add) starting over. I had chalked it up to my hippie brother simply needing a place to crash. And maybe he does. But there's something else too.

Reading this childhood journal of his—really his report from that mental clinic—it's like light bulbs are going off all over the place. Is this what was he thinking when he told those nurses to send me away?

Reading it in my apartment, with him hovering over me with that childlike pain on his face, I couldn't stay. But I couldn't leave it behind. Who knows what he'd do with it? I'm not a thief. I just need to read the whole damn thing.

I pull myself together enough so I don't look like a complete mess walking in to Mitch's office. I'd never admit this to Alden, but I don't have any work to do. Haven't had any work for over a year. Beyond that ugliness that transpired between me and the *M*A*S*H* producers, I've had probably the most serious case of writer's block in the history of the written word. I don't know what my problem is. It's like the page grows eight feet long, my fingers freeze at the keyboard, and whatever I do manage to squeeze out is absolute garbage. I don't need Mitch or anyone else to tell me it sucks. Just last week I destroyed twenty pages of a screenplay proposal. If Mitch hears one more excuse from me, he will probably dissolve our contract—even if it has been almost twenty years running. But God, reading Alden's journal, I'm getting that bubbly-stomach feeling that tells me an idea is brewing. I can't remember the last time I felt so inspired.

"Hey-ya Jerry!" Mitch says over his desk as he hangs up his phone. "Good to see you! Did we have a meeting?" He runs his finger down his planner.

Mitch, my agent, is about ten years my junior and hasn't got a single strand of grey in his full head of dark brown hair. I used to have hair like that, Janine was always quick to remind me. His shirts—collar always open—are perfectly bleached white, which make his teeth look slightly wan. Other than that, he's a decent-looking guy, if you're into Italian types. Some girls go nuts for those dark, intense eyebrows. He's got an excessive amount of energy, which puts me on edge. But he's the best in the business and I'm lucky to have him. I just can't afford to piss him off again.

"No, no," I say. "I won't bother you. I know you're busy. I was hoping to use that spare machine for a while."

"Yours broken?"

I shake my head. "My brother is staying with me for a bit. He needs to use it. Well, I offered to let him use it."

Mitch rubs the back of his neck. "Jerry, we reserve that spare for non-local authors who are on deadline. Who have a *contract*."

I hear the emphasis. But what can I say? It's been a tough dry spell since the divorce. And the *M*A*S*H* fiasco, I don't even want to think about that. Mitch and I haven't been the same since.

Mitch weaves around his desk and closes the door. "Hey-ya," he whispers. "I happen to know it's available for a couple weeks. You could squat until our next out-of-state author comes in."

"Really? Wow, Mitch. That is just great—"

"But! Hold on." He points a hand at me. "You have to work on an approved project. Something I'm going to sell. You can't just sit and tinker."

"Tinker? Mitch, you know me. You know how hard I work."

"Yeah, when it's your own stuff. You work your ass off on whatever interests you. Someone wants you to make war doctors funny and you get so obtuse, you offend the entire studio!" He waves his arms as if to shoo a school of fruit flies. My skin seems to swell on the spot. Weird how shame makes you feel huge when you want to shrink away. Thank goodness the door's closed.

"I can't apologize enough for that," I say to the floor.

"Nah, forget it. Onward and upward. Whatcha got?" He settles back into his chair and taps his fingers on his desk protector, eyeing Alden's binder in my hands.

My stomach drops. I forgot I was still holding it. "Oh, this? This is nothing. I mean it's something, but—"

It's out of my grip and open on his desk before I can object. As Mitch reads, I start to hyperventilate.

Shit!

I tell a half-truth. "Mitch, I have this amazing idea for a screenplay. I'm sure it will sell on the big screen. Maybe we could get Jackie Earle Haley to play the lead—"

Mitch shuts me up with a wave of his hand. I force myself to sit as sweat collects beneath my shirt collar. Mitch's eyes are moving at lightning-agent speed over Alden's binder, but his expression is blank.

He flips to a random page in the middle and reads on. Outside his office door, Nancy the secretary looks in, her eyes question marks. When I go to open the door for her, she retreats, vehemently shaking her head. *Please interrupt*, I want to say. But she knows better, especially when Mitch is reading something.

He flips to the end and reads back a few pages. I strain to see. *I* didn't even get that far. Shit. Poor Alden. I'm so sorry, brother. I'm silently chanting this apology until my tongue goes dry. Maybe I'll sneak out to the bubbler.

"You son of a bitch," Mitch says.

My jaw drops. "Excuse me?"

"Jesus, Mary, and Joseph! So this is what you've been doing? This is what you've been hiding from me?"

"Well, no. Not exactly, see. This is a journal—"

"I know! I can tell! The point of view is extraordinary. A kid. A spoiled brat of a kid with a quirky way of talking. He's funny, this kid. Got an interesting voice. You have a few inconsistencies, I see already, but it might work considering it's written from a kid's perspective. Yes, it just might work." He sucks on the end of his pen, his eyes on the ceiling. "We have to think of a good title. But that will come. How soon can you get this typed up?" He gets up, starts pacing.

My mouth is agape. I should interrupt him, but nothing comes out. It's been so long since he's been excited about something from me—

He claps his hands, giving me a start. "Get the first thirty pages to me by the end of the day and I'll start working on a pitch. We'll send it out tomorrow to Tracy at Little, Brown." He slaps me on the back. "Hell, yeah! You're back, Jerry. I knew you could do it."

He slides back into his chair and starts typing, his lips pursed and eyes narrowing.

I clear my throat. There's got to be a way to save this. "Mitch? I was planning on converting it to a screenplay. And I'm not tied to the names. I was planning on changing them." Jesus, at the very least I *have* to change the names.

He stops typing—he does not like being interrupted—and glares at me. "Wha? What are you saying? Screenplay? No, that won't work at all. You'll lose the voice, which is the best part."

"Yes, but with a narrator—"

"Fuck, no. Please. What you have here is going to work. Don't mess with it. Do what you want with the names. I see you worked your own name in there. A little autobiography in every piece is expected. The title, that's what's important now."

"But—"

Mitch cuts the air like an umpire. "No screenplay. Change names. Find a good title. Got it?"

He starts typing again, bobbing his head with the rhythm of it. I feel like I might throw up. He finally likes something I've got—wants to sell it—and it's *not mine*. What the hell am I going to do?

I start to back out of the office. "Hey-ya, don't forget your binder, Jerry." Mitch hands it over with his signature wink. "That's gold right there."

My fingers start tingling when I take it. I smile my best, tucking it under my arm. The room feels like it's moving, but I walk out with purpose, hugging that thing to my side like it *is* solid gold as I take a long drink from the bubbler. I nod hello to Nancy on my way to the spare machine in the cubicle behind her. I crack my knuckles over the keyboard. And exhale.

Okay, I had wanted to use it for inspiration. I didn't lie to Mitch; I do have an idea for a screenplay. Boy gets kicked out of prep school, embarks on pilgrimage through New York City on a solo, dramatic, coming-of-age journey. It would work as a film, right? But that's not Mitch's vision. Mitch wants it as is, basically. Just wants me to type it up. Simple. Do I have a choice? Turn it into something positive, is what I said to Alden. So, maybe this is how it's supposed to go.

Mitch probably won't be able to sell it. Even if he does, it's a long shot it will even go anywhere. I mean, does anyone read anymore? Doesn't everyone just go to the movies?

I turn to the last page of Alden's journal, the last line: "*It's funny. Don't ever tell anybody anything. If you do, you start missing everybody.*"

Goose bumps rise on my arms. Hell. This journal was meant to be read. If Alden doesn't want to make that happen, someone should. And if I do it, maybe it will save my pitiful career. It *can* become something positive. For everyone.

Chapter 3
Fiona

As I hold the thermometer tip under my tongue, I'm reminded of those rare early mornings when my head felt full of lava and would not budge off the pillow. Mom would sit by my waist, keeping her eyes on her wristwatch. Sometimes I'd curl around her sturdy figure, feeling the sheet stretch against my hips, and luxuriate in a secret hug. Unlike my grammar-school classmates, I never liked sick days. Rather than hold the thermometer near a light bulb, I'd suck cool air between my lips that were surreptitiously loose around the glass tube. It would be ages before the verdict was in. Mom would lay the back of her hand against my cheek, her eyes as even as a registered nurse's, and announce I would have to miss school. Then, it would descend upon me: a huge empty mass of ineffectual time, which I would have to wade through like a flea stuck in molasses.

Taking my own temperature is strange, especially when I feel better than well. Rather than watch the clock, I take to plucking my eyebrows, clicking the thermometer against the mirror as I lean into it. I wouldn't dare try any light bulb antics, no matter how desperate I am to see a delta of a few degrees. Just a line or two—enough to let me know my body is working on something. My lips are pursed so tightly around the thing, they nearly go numb by the end of it, when I find myself stretching my lips like an opera singer doing warm-ups.

Normal. Maybe a tenth higher.

I shake the mercury down and rinse off the tip. Tomorrow, maybe.

David and I have been trying to get pregnant for three years now. All those years of being careful—jeepers, I could've just relaxed. Who knew it would be this hard? When my period comes and I'm reminded we've failed again, David holds me as I cry. He has agreed to see a doctor after another few months of trying. In the meantime, I'm sick with worry. What if there is a serious problem? What if we can't conceive?

Lately, I've been wondering what really happened with Jerry and Janine. Mom told me only bits after the tragedy, and I respected their privacy. But now, I want all the details: warning signs, doctor visits. I'm tempted to reach out to Jerry, but he's not like Alden. Ever since I can remember, Jerry's been cold to me—and I'm not sure why. To Alden, too. I'm hoping they will become closer now that they live together. There I go, now I'm worrying again.

Back in the kitchen, I put the kettle on for tea and start the morning's tedium. When I quit my job shortly after David and I got married, I expected pregnancy—and then motherhood—to keep me busy. I hadn't thought that by ten every morning, after logging the morning's temperature, I would be twiddling my thumbs. But that's what happens when the only responsibility of your day is to clean up after breakfast. And then there's that wide yawn of time before dinner preparations. I've read more books in the last two years than I've read in my entire life.

At least I have a distraction today: my dear friend Linda needs my help preparing for a job interview. We meet in an hour down at a coffee shop on Mass. Ave. I'm surprised by my eagerness for this casual meeting. I'm not lonely, not really. It's just that the house is so empty all day.

As I wait for the water to boil, I plan the next hour. Should I sort spices or organize Tupperware? There is that story Alden wrote about poor Allie, its pages fanning out on the sideboard as if trying to make an escape. Oh, Alden, my dear brother. Alden channeling Allie's sweet little voice—letting him tell his own story. It's like he wanted to tackle the source of his sadness, straight on. I'm honored he wants me to read it. And I do want to help him. I hope I can, but it's hard for me.

What do I remember about Allie? When he asked me that point-blank while he was writing, I told him nothing specific came to mind. But I do remember that time. I was seven—plenty old enough to capture clear memories. Just not of Allie, even though he bridged the six-year gap between me and Alden. Perhaps because my ovaries are throbbing for a baby, I can't help but think of Mother whenever I try to remember my deceased brother.

The kettle sings and I ceremoniously fix my cup of tea, sifting through my selection of tea bags and weighing the benefits of lemon versus milk. I choose the latter only to hurry the cooling process. I cradle the mug in my hands and breathe in the tangy vapor of steeping tea. I find myself standing before the sideboard, sighing at Alden's binder of photocopied, hand-written pages. There is no avoiding it anymore. I pick up Alden's story, settle into the kitchen chair that faces the magnolia tree out the bay window, and start—

Phone ringing! I'm saved.

"Fee, it's Linda! There's a change-up. I could only get into the salon at, like, the exact time I'm supposed to meet you for coffee. And I totally want my highlights to look perfect for this interview."

Linda's got the most enviable hair on the planet. Seriously, Farrah herself would fawn over the perfectly frosted, feathered locks. "Oh—"

"I don't suppose we could meet another time? Or maybe do it over the phone?"

I nearly deflate from disappointment. "Yeah, sure—"

"I mean, I'm interviewing for a job in Human Resources. That's what I do. Doesn't it seem, like, superfluous to interview me? I mean, I am the one who will be doing interviews in the future…"

"All the more reason—"

A sigh. "Right. You're right. Especially since this would be a step up."

"Is it? A promotion? How exciting!"

"Well, it's got a PR component. That's why I wanted to talk with you."

"Oh?" Envy fills me.

"Well, I would do the contracts, but then hire the writer. Probably freelance."

"Right." My heart's thumping. Me, me, me! I want to say. Freelance, permanent, anything! "What about strategy?"

Linda laughs. "I'll leave that to my boss!"

"You might want to have some ideas for tomorrow. Research the company as best you can—"

"Fee, really. How hard is it going to be to come up with a strategy to sell candy?"

"Candy?"

"Yeah. The company is McGarry Sweets."

"The one in Cambridge?"

"That's the one. Near MIT."

Envy strikes again. Linda will essentially be soaking up the college experience once more—on her lunch breaks. Not just any college. MIT! She's going to get smarter simply from osmosis.

She tries to cancel our meeting, assuming it's a burden for me. But I insist. She suggests meeting later in the afternoon, and even though that's when I usually cat-nap on the window seat—when did I become such an old lady?—I agree.

"Three o'clock it is," I say.

The conversation with Linda has made me stronger, somehow. I reheat my tea in the microwave, pick up Alden's story, and settle in my chair, taking a deep breath in as I start to read.

Do you know what you can build with Legos? Absolutely anything! Mom started bringing them in—all sizes. It's not that I'd never played with Legos before. But now that I'm stuck in bed and have all the time in the world. Well, almost. ...I can try all kinds of things. You should see what I'm building now! The Edinburgh Cathedral. That's right. The one in Scotland. And no, I've never been there. But I'm getting it right. I mean, sometimes I have to explain a mansard roof or the exact angle of a dormer, but I'm getting it mostly right just by sight. I tell you. They can pump me with all the chemicals in the world, but nothing makes me feel better than getting a Lego project done. Is that weird? My room is full of bright colored ships and skyscrapers and fighter jets. I even made one of the hospital where I'm hanging out (it was an uninspired day. Ha!). My favorite was when I built a model of our camp in Maine, though. It was right on. Even the little awning over the back door and the front porch that wraps around one side. I gave it to Mom for Mother's Day, even though she didn't much feel like celebrating. But she loved it! She said she'd keep it until the day she died. I think it was just a figure of speech. But I made her shake on it, which made her cry happy tears. Mom's been crying a lot lately. Happy tears are my favorite though. Hers too.

Mom. The word reads like a sigh.

It's like the floor has fallen out and I'm immovable in free fall. Grief for my mother threatens to suffocate me, whenever I am reminded she is gone. What a terribly appropriate word: gone. And to where? While I'm unable to cling to a soothing picture of afterlife for her, I am equally unwilling to wait for my subconscious to place her in my dreams. So she remains clouded in my grief, in my inadequate memories. I stare out at the brown leaves of the magnolia tree and try to recall the magnificent white blooms that have disappeared with the chill of autumn. I wait for tears to break the knot in my chest. Why does it feel so new, even five years later?

It's true that wanting my own children makes me miss her more than ever. She never got to meet David, which breaks my heart. But thank goodness she was spared seeing Dad marry again and move to Arizona! And Jerry's divorce and debilitating sadness. She never did worry about me or Jerry, though. Her concern, after Allie died, was reserved for Alden.

The phone rings again, giving me a start. It's Alden.

"Two days in a row," I say. "Wow. I am honored."

"Do you have a minute? I just hoped we could, y'know, pick up from where we left off yesterday." He wants to talk about his story.

I clear my throat, hoping to reset my mind. "Yes. Well, I'm meeting Linda soon. She's got an interview tomorrow. You remember Linda, don't you? She was one of my bridesmaids."

"Right on. You go ahead. Maybe I can call you later?"

"Yes, do."

But there is his story splayed before me, his handwriting possessing all the hope of a second grader learning proper penmanship. And I do have loads of time.

Alden's saying something now and although I'm not listening, I can feel his eagerness. I breathe in, and through what must be a subconscious loophole, I think I smell magnolia.

"Actually, I do have a few minutes. I mean, while it's fresh in my mind…"

Chapter 4
Jerry

What is done cannot be undone.

(You know it can't be good when I start quoting *Macbeth*.)

I'm driving home from the office, having delivered another fifty perfect pages to Mitch. He's got about three quarters of it now, I think. We decided on a title, *The Phony Rebel*, which I personally abhor. But Mitch was all wound up about it, since the word "phony" appears dozens of times in the piece. "It describes your protagonist to a T!" he said, and scratched it on the chalkboard in his office and gazed at it like it was scripture.

It's late—about seven—when I enter my apartment. The whole place smells like weed and Lennon is crooning out *Strawberry Fields Forever* from my boom box. Alden's there on the couch with a bag of chips in his lap, keeping rhythm on the coffee table with his bare feet.

"Good tune," I say. Like so much else about Alden, I'd forgotten we both loved the Beatles. Janine was a huge fan, too. She had a crush on George, but she would never admit to it.

"Yo brotha. How was work?" he says, rolling his eyes toward me. He's not totally stoned, I can tell. But he looks pathetic, wearing that stained Dylan shirt again. I rub my bald spot as I consider Alden's hair. He always had it high and tight growing up—so short I barely knew its true reddish-blonde color. Fiona told me that he grew dreadlocks in San Diego—his hippie days. Red dreads. What a stereotype. But now it's this weird in-between thing. It looks like a shag rug made for a little girl's room.

I hang my jacket in the closet. Hopefully it won't pick up the weed smell in there. Alden follows me into the kitchen and straddles a chair.

"Whassup?" he says.

Suddenly, it all comes back. What I've been up to. What I'm doing. After working on his journal for a few days, I had myself convinced it had nothing to do with him. Just a project. Well, mostly convinced. Not enough to bring it inside. It's out in my trunk right now. Alden's casual gaze on me feels like fire. My face is burning.

"Hey," I say, and open the freezer. The cold feels good. I don't even care that he ate all my ice cream.

"Sorry I ate all your ice cream, brotha."

"That's okay." I pull out a frozen pizza and click on the oven to preheat. "Want some pizza?"

"Starving!" Alden says, and gives me this huge smile. He's happy I'm home. Makes me feel like even more of a schmuck.

I hand him a Coke and crack one open for myself. I wish I had some beer.

"So," I say. "How did it go today? How's it coming along with the machine?"

"That thing is so cool. I'm getting it down so fast. It would be faster, too, but I'm editing as I go. Kind of rewriting parts."

"That's good. Right. That's what you should do."

"Is that what you do?"

My stomach hollows out. "Sure. Yeah. I'm always editing, you know."

Alden starts drumming the table, singing along to *Baby, You're a Rich Man.*

"You like the Beatles?" he asks.

"You don't have to be a hippie to appreciate good music," I say.

"Revolutionary music," he corrects me. "Yo, you're not calling me a flower child, are you?"

"No way," I say, surrendering my hands. It's true. If he was a hippie ten years ago, he's certainly not anymore. He wouldn't be living here if—

"Not anymore," he says, laughing.

"You said it. I didn't."

Track switches to *All You Need is Love.* I'm sure it wasn't Lennon's intention but this song has always made me sad for some reason, even when Janine and I were together and things were good. Huh. I'm staring at the wall trying to remember when things were good when Alden changes the subject.

"So. I thought we could brainstorm a little tonight. You can fill me in on how you remember ol' Allie. I haven't interviewed you yet. I mean, you were much older when he died, so you must remember everything."

"Of course." It's the least I can do, right? I can relive that awful time. I can do that for Alden.

Alden clicks the can with his fingernails. "So, I noticed my journal is gone. Been gone a few days now."

"Huh?" Shit. "Oh, yeah." I can feel the start of a headache smack in the middle of my brain, spreading like tree roots.

"So, where is it?" He chuckles, more incredulous than jolly.

The timer goes off. "Oh, I have it," I say, as I busy myself at the oven—which isn't a lie. In response, he holds his arms out, like *What gives?* I try to ignore him.

"Not cool, Jerr."

"Thought I'd get it away from you since it seemed to, well, dredge up stuff."

Alden looks at me from the sides of his eyes, like a cat. A ticked cat. Then he shakes his head.

"Just give it back, okay? It doesn't need to be anywhere but in with all my other childhood shit."

"Sure thing," I say. I cut the pizza while Alden flips the cassette tape to side one of *Magical Mystery Tour*.

We're quiet while we eat, listening to the Beatles, playing much louder than my usual. Tonight, though, I am grateful for this diversion. We eat the whole pie and go through another couple Cokes.

"I want to let you know," Alden says with a mouth full of pepperoni. "I'm not sitting around all day smoking chonger."

"I know."

"Just a hit at the end of the day. A reward." Alden grins like a schoolboy trying to please his teacher. I force myself to smile back. I want to tell him to do it somewhere else, out of my apartment, even open my mouth to start to say it. But I stop, and instead make a big deal about stretching.

"I'm exhausted," I say. "Can we talk about Allie tomorrow or something? I'm going to hit the hay."

Alden nods as he chews his last crust. I leave before he can say anything else, about Allie, or his journal, or smoking dope. All the garbage sits on the table. The music is still blaring. I don't care. I just want to be alone.

But then. In the dark the demons come. Damn, I'm a bunch of clichés today. My shame moves over to make room; now I'm haunted. He stays away long enough for me to brush my teeth and change and slide under the comforter. But as soon as the light is off, Allie's there.

Allie. That firecracker hair and freckles so big you could see them across the room. What a doll he was, and so smart. Before he was able to read and write, he would get a pencil or a crayon and paper and *demand* I show him how to write letters. He'd always ask when I was busy with my own homework or watching television or something. But I would indulge him most of the time. And I had to show him in the proper order, because he knew the alphabet song. God, he must have been about three or four then; I was probably twelve. And those magnetic letters on the fridge. "Jerry, how do you spell 'train'?" He would bug me until I stopped what I was doing and showed him. Made me late for a track meet once. Boy, I was sore about that. But the look on his face after I showed him—pure awe. He'd give me this big, baby-teeth smile and say the word again and again, running his finger over the bright colored letters as if he'd solved a puzzle. I didn't know enough to appreciate that.

One morning our mother took all those letters off the fridge to clean it, and Allie came in—still wearing his pajamas—and started wailing. His face turned bright red under his freckles, fat tears running over them. His cries warbled his words. Mom kept asking if he hurt himself and he just kept pointing at the fridge. Mom opened it and offered him milk and yogurt and whatever else she saw in there. Alden was the one who figured it out. "The letters, Mom. He wants the letters. Where'd they go?" You should've seen how fast Mom put those letters back on that fridge.

I was already abroad with the military when we found out he was sick. No one's mom calls active barracks. So when Lieutenant Peters pulled me in for a phone call that Wednesday afternoon, I knew something was wrong. Mom could barely get it out. She kept whispering the word, as if she couldn't say it aloud. There was all this background noise—guys shouting and engines roaring and helicopters walloping. "Allie's got what?" I asked, blocking my other ear with my thumb.

"Leukemia!" she yelled, and it was like the word was a trigger. She started bawling, hysterical. Had to give the phone to Dad. But all my words were gone. Dad told me not to rush home because they were planning on a long, arduous recovery regimen. He sounded like Lieutenant Peters, very businesslike. Even though he didn't ask, I managed a visit home a few months later. It sounds awful to say but I almost wished I hadn't. Allie just wasn't Allie anymore. His firecracker hair was gone, leaving a pale helmet-looking shape around his freckles. He was so skinny, with these dark craters under his eyes. He was all hooked up to IVs and machines, like his body was at war. He smiled when he saw me, but didn't have the strength to talk. I had brought his favorite candy, red licorice, as a gift—which he couldn't eat. I kissed his bald head and told him I'd be back soon. And even though I had planned to be home for two weeks, I arranged my flight out the next day. I know. That's what's ugly. But I knew if I never saw him again, I'd at least remember him as *him*, with his bright red hair. And bugging me to show him letters and words. And that big baby-teeth smile. I did go back the next morning to say goodbye, though. That was March. He died sometime in the middle of July.

It's weird. I can't remember the in-between. After he started kindergarten and I was in high school, I barely remember talking to him or even hanging out watching television, although I'm sure we must have. I just can't find it.

Or I couldn't...until I found Alden's journal. It's like a lens into the workings of a family I had never known— yet it was mine.

My gut feels like it's boiling. I clench my whole body in anger. First, Allie gets sick and dies while I'm overseas. Then Alden gets sick and rejects me. Then Fiona nearly destroys my career. Why wasn't I part of this family? It's like I've been sabotaged. Or sacrificed.

After two hours I'm still awake. I take some cough syrup, enough to finally knock me out. As I drift off, I force myself to think about something else. Janine is there next to me. I can feel her warmth. I fall asleep sort of happy. Dumb happy.

Chapter 5
Alden

Every morning, Jerry splits super early before I get up. Every night when he gets back, I ask him for my goddam journal. And every time, he plays dumb. Fucking kid. His latest? My journal—the black binder—is acting as a bookend at his office, and if he takes it down the whole row of books will tumble like dominoes. What a story. Totally bogue. I might have to march into his office and take the goddam thing myself if he doesn't give it back soon. Been a whole week.

Whatever. I try not to think about it, or the words inside.

Even though Jerry is gone and I have the place to myself, I go to Mobil first thing. It's my routine. Clear my head before getting to work on *Allie*. It's a stellar morning. No wind. Overcast. Sleepy. Even the traffic seems calm. I'm gravy when I go through the door and hear the bell jangle against it.

Then I get in an even better mood.

Bracelets isn't there. A different girl is, and she is a goddess. Foxy lady. The door shuts—pushing me in, like—and I just stare at her. She glances up and smiles— a flash of white—then peers down at something on the counter. A magazine maybe. She's got caramel skin and a plump little pucker. Tight black curls in a wild crown framing her round, dimpled face.

"Hi," I say. Then, like a total doofus: "Where's Bracelets?"

Maybe I don't sound so geeky, because she cracks up, covering her mouth, shy-like. I chuckle and fiddle with a box of Marlboros.

"She's off, I take it?" I can't help it. I get a girl laughing and I swear I become a total Casanova.

Goddess nods and her curls bounce around. Adorable. I put my Marlboros on the counter and point to the warming trays. "Those egg sandwiches grody or no?"

Goddess shrugs, still kind of giggling.

"So, are you able to speak? Because I'm totally cool with sign language. Let's get the groove on." I start gesticulating like a madman. She goes bananas then, stomping and covering her mouth. Why do girls act embarrassed when they laugh? It's so cute, though, the way Goddess does it. She finally chills and says, "We have egg and cheese, and ham, egg and cheese."

"She speaks!" I pretend to stumble back, wide-eyed. She cracks up again.

"I hear the ham is worth it," she says. That sweet caramel skin blushes and I'm jonesing. I could eat her up for breakfast.

"Ham it is then," I say. I'm out of jokes.

She rings me up and I hand over the moolah. I guess I'm supposed to split but there isn't anyone else in there and I'm scoping on Goddess. For real.

"I'm Alden."

"Kyra. But my friends call me Kiki."

I hold out my hand and give her my killer smile. "Hey Sunshine. It's official. We're pals, Kiki, whether you like it or not."

She laughs. "Oh really?"

A lady comes in—barges in actually—and orders a coffee. That kills me. Not only were Kiki and I obviously getting into it, but the coffee here is self-serve. Kiki is super nice, though. Comes around the counter and pumps a few ounces into a Styrofoam cup for the lady. Even asks if she prefers milk or cream, sugar or Sweet'N Low. She stirs it with one of those skinny wooden sticks and tops it with a plastic lid. It only takes a few minutes, but I'm grateful because I can check out Kiki's banging figure.

Brick. House. Voluptuous and a little thicker than what I'm used to. Like a warm bagel. Delectable.

The lady is in a colossal hurry all of a sudden and kinda pushes me out of the way. I step aside like a gentleman, and wait my turn for Kiki's attention. What happens, though, is it starts to pick up in that Mobil, gets totally busy. Like a Greyhound unloaded out front. Kiki's real focused and polite to everyone. And I know I need to split. I don't want to. But I do.

I figure I'll call Fiona, and maybe come back, assuming the place chills out. En route to the pay phone, I finger-comb my hair and consider a haircut. A beautiful girl will do that to you. Make you think about a haircut.

"Two days in a row," Fiona says after hearing my voice. "Wow. I am honored."

"Do you have a minute? I just hoped we could, y'know, pick up from where we left off yesterday."

"Yes. Well, I'm meeting Linda soon. She's got an interview tomorrow. You remember Linda, don't you?"

I don't.

"She was one of my bridesmaids."

My stomach goes junky again, because of course I can only remember one bridesmaid. Goddam, am I not going to be able to talk to my little sister—my favorite person in the whole world—ever again?

"Right on. You go ahead. Maybe I can call you later?"

"Yes, do." Fiona is always saying grandmotherly things like "yes, do." I think it's sweet as hell. She would never be insincere. Fiona is totally solid. Always has been.

"Okay. I'll try you this afternoon—"

"Actually," she says, and her voice gets faint, like she's moving away from the phone. Then she's back. "I do have a few minutes. I mean, while it's fresh in my mind."

"Yeah? Groovy." I wish I had a notebook or something. I can tell she's going to give me something heavy.

She takes this big, deep breath. "First of all, I'm so proud of you, Alden. You've worked so hard on this. I can't believe you wrote a whole novel! Not many people can say they've done that."

I'm waiting through her pleasantries. She's being nice, but I want the lowdown.

"I guess…I just have a few questions."

"Word." I chew this hangnail on my thumb. Nasty habit.

"So, well. As I've told you, I don't really remember Allie much, unfortunately. But I really enjoy getting to know him through your book. It means a lot to me, personally."

"Yeah, I was wondering if it brought you back at all. You get me? Like, Sundays at the park with Allie?"

"I know," she says in a voice that sounds like an apology. "You asked me about that before. The sailboat—"

"Yes! You were just a wee babe, but you had, like, massive ears."

Fiona laughs.

"I'm talking metaphorically, sis."

"I know, I know. I guess I didn't want to miss anything important, as if everything my big brothers said would be."

"So, you remember then?"

"Well, no. Not really. I recall moments, as if they were captured by a photograph. I remember his smile. His hair, of course. But details about what he used to do and bits of conversation aren't there. But, what I was going to ask…about Allie…"

She trails off, and I can't wait. "What? What's up?"

"Were you trying to make him some sort of superhero?"

I bust a gut. "No!"

"I'm sorry," she says. "Not a superhero. I meant a person with super powers."

That gives me pause. She does get it. "Mystical," I say. "Yeah, I was."

She makes a thinking noise, a nice hum. I can tell she's trying to remember something. "Like that time when he could sense what was going to happen to that plane," she says. "And he managed to stop Mom and Dad from getting on that flight for their golf trip in North Carolina.

I had heard that story before, although Mom didn't credit Allie quite so much. But the way you captured Allie's intuition. And his innocence. That was amazing."

No joke; I have tears in my eyes. "So you dig it, then?"

"Oh, Alden. Yes. But—"

"What?"

Another deep breath. "It made me sad, Alden."

"Of course it made you sad. Poor Allie died when he was *eleven*. What a nightmare! Who wouldn't be sad about that?"

"No, Alden." She's apologizing again. "I was sad...for you."

"Me?" That totally spins me.

"Yeah. Are you okay?" The way she says it, it's like no matter what I say I won't convince her that I am. It makes me wiggly inside, like I'm a boat on a rippling sea. I just want off now. "So, if there's a part where you think I'm jiving or you just don't get it, let me know," I say in a rush. "That stuff totally helps."

"Sure, sweetie. I took some notes. Small things, really. Grammar mostly. Do you want me to send them to Jerry's?"

Sweetie. She must know Teresa used to call me that. My gut twists and I say, "That would be killer. Tell Linda good luck. Catch ya." And I hang up.

The last thing I feel like doing is going back into the Mobil to scope on Kiki. I'm deflated, can't find my high from earlier. I mean, I'm glad Fiona gave me the 411. I just wish it was more—I don't know—glowing, I guess. Maybe not. That wouldn't really help. But what she did give me—I'm not sure what to do with it. She's sad for *me*? Where the hell is that coming from? I'm barely *in* the book. I totally wrote it that way on purpose. When I chill out some, I'll have to ask her exactly why she got that impression, because that's definitely not what I'm going for.

Hope Jerry's not home. I just want to put my head down and get to work. I take the same route back as I did the other day and pass the abandoned baseball field. The ol' benches call my name, so I pop a squat and eat my egg sandwich. The sun feels fab as I tilt my face to it. But then I hear it again, and I almost choke on a piece of ham. *Sweetie.* But it's just in my head. I guess now is when I fill you in. I might as well.

I met Teresa at Fiona and Dave's wedding. Well, scratch that. I actually met her at Boston College when I visited Fiona once, but I didn't *notice* her until Fiona's wedding. All bridesmaids wore these teal numbers, big poofy gowns. Teresa was one of the four. I don't remember the other three, honestly. All I know is, Teresa's eyes were the most beautiful green color I had ever seen. Like early spring leaves—when they're almost gold. Like how Robert Frost described it in that poem. As soon as I got a good look at those eyes, I was a goner. We danced a few numbers. She could move, which didn't hurt matters. She smelled like vanilla. The band was lousy, but big Dave and I didn't share musical tastes, so. Anyway, when I complimented her green eyes, she shooed me and said, "They're not green. They're brown!" She said "brown" like it was shit. But she was serious. She totally didn't think her eyes were green. I swear I fell in love with her right then. I wasn't going to let her go another minute not knowing, though.

I snuck her into the ladies room, took her to the mirror so she could see her honest-to-God eye color. You should've seen her face. She stared at her reflection for the longest time, barely blinking, her mouth a little open. Her lipstick had faded and her hairdo was coming out from all that dancing, but she looked sweet. Natural. She was pretty—not a total fox as they say, but there was something about her. Something better. More real. I checked out her whole face. It was a really decent shape, round forehead and a soft bulge to her cheeks. There was a dusting of freckles under her makeup. I stared right at her, and I could because she was distracted. It was like she'd never seen her own eyes. Then, she locked those golden eyes on me. It felt like we stood there for an hour, just staring at each other. Then, she put her hand on my face. It was probably the softest skin I'd ever come into contact with. I can't tell you what kind of powers she must've had but it was like a bolt shot through me. "Thank you," she said, and beat it out of there. I didn't move. I could still feel a warm spot on my cheek. I stayed on in the goddam ladies room until big Dave's aunt walked in with a run in her stocking. Scared the hell out of her. Hell, I jumped too. I had forgotten where I was. A beautiful moment can do that to you.

We were together after that. And it was true, what she said. Her eyes were really brown. Every once in a while if we sat by a window at a diner or on a bus, the natural light would make her eyes shine that forest gold I told you about. But most of the time they were brown. Still, a nice brown. But it was cool. It was like I had a secret with her.

We were supposed to get married. Have kids. Follow the path. I can't even tell you what happened.

I feel about as fulfilled as this ballpark right now. Time to blow this taco stand.

Lucky me. Jerry's gone when I get in. I shuck off my kicks and watch a little news. But then I get sucked into this true story of a football player who battled cancer and won, and then came back out to play before all his hair grew in again. And he was better than ever. Coach said he played with more heart. They made this big deal about his hair growing in different. Curly. They say that it sometimes happens with cancer survivors. The story just about kills me. I mean, I have to wipe tears off my goddam cheeks. The heavy background music doesn't help. Geez, they really know how to tug at your heartstrings. I get that this is a totally awesome outcome for this guy, but all I can do is think of Allie, whether his hair would've grown in different. If it had a chance to.

I click off the boob tube and decide to take a shower. Sometimes I think better under a rush of hot water. I can't get Allie's hair out of my mind, though, which makes me think of Fiona's hair when she was a kid. I'm still dripping from the shower when I search the closet in Jerry's spare room for an old photo album so I can see it—the color. Just the brightest, most far-out red. Neither one of them loved it. Fiona knows how to work hers now, though. Besides it's changed, like it's matured along with her. Now it's this dark auburn shade other chicks go bananas for.

I find a thick forest-green album of Jerry and Janine's vacation to Aruba or somewhere beachy. One photo catches my eye. Jerry's beaming at the camera, just beaming, and Janine has her hand near his face, her fingers curled around his ear. And she's looking at him with this half smile, like she's thinking of something else. I can't stop looking at this pic, see, because it seems to explain why they called it quits. I'm sure to you they would look like a sweet, happy couple. But I can see it in her eyes; she's not totally there with Jerry. She's already halfway gone.

I slam the book away and dress in haste. Suddenly it's way too quiet in the apartment. I turn on *Sgt. Pepper*. Loud. Good ol' "Penny Lane." I sing along at the top of my lungs. Boo-yah! I sit down at the machine, the tunes full tilt, and start typing with my pointers. I'm totally fast now. Just cruising. I crank out two chapters lickety-split. I decide to stretch my legs and print out what I have so far.

The sound of the printing is driving me crazy, so I venture out to see if Jerry's got any Coke. Something tells me I drank his last. And I'm right.

I toy with the idea of heading to Mobil again, but instead I decide to go in the other direction. I think I saw a pharmacy that way.

It's a stellar day. Fog has burned off and the air feels light and breezy. Fab walking weather. After a few blocks, I toke my doobie. Just one hit. I carefully put it out under my kicks and save the roach for later, back in the box of smokes. Good thing it's tucked away too, because I turn the next corner and—*bam!*—everything's busy, like city-busy. Traffic, people. Even the buildings change. More storefronts and stuff. I have no idea where I am except on Cantrell Avenue. It doesn't bother me, but it is awfully hectic suddenly. I duck into a newsstand just to get my bearings, get out of people's way.

The clerk is looking at me like I'm tripping so I buy another pack of squares with my Coke, even though I have Marlboros in my pocket. Then he gives me the hairy eyeball when I go to light up. So, I'm back outside before I know it. I'm smoking and watching all the men in suits rush to their next appointment. Across the street there is a totally officious-looking building. That's probably where all these guys in suits are headed. Then I start seeing people in scrubs—mostly women in scrubs. My heart picks up and I stamp out my smoke. I walk to the corner so I can see the sign.

Hot dog! It couldn't have worked out better if I planned it. Just a few blocks away. Rue Phillip's Oncology Clinic.

I tuck in my shirt as I walk through the glass doors.

Chapter 6
Fiona

The best part about helping a friend get a job is having her return the favor. As soon as Linda was hired as HR coordinator for McGarry Sweets, she convinced them to hire me for the company's PR, which will be my first legitimate freelance gig. When I'd considered freelancing, I had mistakenly thought projects would simply land in my lap. I hadn't realized how much effort it takes to market yourself, which does not come naturally to me. Let me praise others all day long; I'm uncomfortable promoting myself in any context. Hopefully, Linda took care of that for me today.

I'm driving to meet Linda and her boss, my briefcase on the passenger seat holding the client questionnaire that will help me craft the perfect message. I've been such a nest of nerves, I didn't eat breakfast. I almost didn't answer the phone when Alden called. Oh, Alden. Dear brother. Every time we talk I can feel his pain over Teresa. I don't have the heart to tell him about her and Chad.

I never worried about my brothers until I was married. Now I'm driving my husband crazy worrying about Jerry and Alden—each for separate reasons. At least they've had each other these last few months, unlikely roommates though they are. Although just to think of how that place must smell... David thinks I'm being unnecessarily overprotective. "They're grown men," he tells me. I know. I can't help it. Since Mom died, I am the mom now. At least in the figurative sense. How ironic.

But I must count my blessings. I am so lucky to have found David. I took everyone's advice and waited for the right man, marrying at the age of twenty-nine, when most women were already changing diapers. I was working at Lotham and Greenstein, and we had just acquired a new client: a fast-moving Boston agency that specialized in business-to-business marketing. David worked in their finance department and stumbled into the wrong meeting—my meeting. I still blush when I think of it.

David walked in, a hint of annoyance in his eyes as he took a seat. Everyone knew he was in the wrong room, and not four minutes into the presentation, David had figured it out. I didn't know his position in the company then, so I couldn't help him, but I wanted to so badly. He looked so vulnerable: puffing out his cheeks with each breath, moisture wetting the soft pale hair on his forehead. He kept wiping around the bridge of his glasses. He had this endearing, gentle way about him, like a little boy. From across the table, I could see the prominent mole on his chin and I fleetingly wondered if he had difficulty shaving around it. I also noticed his eyes: a calm blue, but a little red from lack of sleep. He glanced up, catching my eye for a millisecond. He must've seen something there.

"I'm sorry," he said, tapping the conference table with his legal pad. "You don't look like insurance folk. I must be in the wrong meeting. How embarrassing."

After one awkward beat of silence, the presentation continued. David exited swiftly with no further apology, looking back momentarily. We still argue about it, but I will swear to my grave that he winked at me on his way out that door. He says it was a muscle spasm.

After the meeting, on the way to my car, I had my briefcase tucked under my arm and was reapplying my lipstick when I felt someone behind me. A sixth sense, David says now. I turned around, holding my lipstick in mid-air, having only covered my top lip. I was so preoccupied with my own discomfiture I barely understood he meant to ask me on a date.

I don't remember how I gave him my number or whether I finished applying my lipstick. But it didn't matter. Somehow I knew right then, before we even went out. He would be the one.

I pull up to Linda's new office, double-check the address to make sure. I'm relieved when I realize I'm early. I refresh my lipstick in the rearview and see a swab of purple on my teeth! I smudge it out with my finger, and my nerves start going again. I decide it's better to wait in the lobby than drive myself crazy in the car. I grab my briefcase and head in.

I'm on my second glass of chardonnay when David comes home. It's dark in the kitchen except for the apple-cinnamon scented candle I'm staring at somewhat trance-like when I hear the door open. Usually I'm on my feet at the door, throwing my arms around his neck, smelling his starchy, after-work smell. But tonight I stay seated, trying not to cry.

He steps softly into the kitchen. "It didn't go well, I gather?"

His arms are around me. I blubber messily into his collar, trying to explain. But it comes out all muddled. *Peanuts* grown-up talk.

"Slow down," he says. "It's okay. Whatever happened, it's okay."

That calms me a bit. David waits beside me, patting my forearm until my breathing settles.

"It was awful," I say. "He was obviously just doing her a favor, Linda's boss. He didn't have any intention of hiring me. If he had laughed at my questionnaire it would've been better. But he scowled at it."

David winces in sympathy. I hand him my questionnaire. He reads it carefully, although he's read it before. He fingers the paisley stamp I used to embellish the margins. I can read his mind.

"I thought it looked boring without any…decoration."

He shrugs.

"You think it looks juvenile."

"No—"

"Yes you do. It does! It's distracting. Why did I bother fancying it up? I should've just had the questions in big bold typeface. Or maybe I should've just conducted it as an interview and not given him any handout at all." I slurp my wine uncharacteristically. It goes down easily tonight.

"Fiona, the border doesn't matter. If he didn't like it, fine. But if he couldn't see past it and know that these are smart questions he will have to answer…"

"I know! What a prick."

David nearly flinches, then bursts out laughing. It may be the first time he's heard me curse.

53

"He is! That McGarry character. Todd or Tom or whatever his name is. Roly-poly bastard is what he is."

David's laughing hard now. He's got the singular best laugh on the planet: a little hoarse and squeaky, but one hundred percent sincere. He takes off his glasses and wipes his eyes. He goes to get his own wine glass, pouring some for himself, refilling mine.

"That'll be number three," I warn him, though it's just for show. To be honest, getting a little tipsy doesn't sound like the worst idea. "He was so rude, David! You should've seen him. He was blatantly flirting with Linda right in front of me. And after scowling at my questionnaire, I swear I think he winked at her."

David nearly chokes on his wine. "What's with you and the winking, Fiona? You always think you see people winking. Maybe it was a twitch."

"Or a muscle spasm?"

"No, probably a twitch."

I squeeze David's hand three times: *I love you.* He squeezes three times back. We're both grinning. The world is put right. I rest my calves on his lap and he massages them under my sweatpants.

"Linda took me out to lunch after. She kept apologizing. It was so humiliating."

"What did you say?"

"I played it off as no big deal. I told her I had plenty of other work."

"You do have work. You have our newsletter."

I twirl my finger in the air. David's company's bi-weekly newsletter—internal communication—is not my favorite type of PR.

"Then Linda offered to take me shopping. For clothes." I look down at my ensemble. Navy cardigan over an off-white turtleneck, now paired with the sweatpants I'd pulled on to replace the uncomfortable skirt and panty hose. "Do you think I'm a sloppy dresser?"

"No."

I know him. "But?"

"No, you always look good, Fiona. With your figure, you make anything look good. I would never say 'sloppy.' I would say 'comfortable.'"

For some reason, this doesn't bother me. I'm sure other wives would be offended. But the thing is, I *am* a comfortable dresser. Always have been. Fashion bores me. Shopping too. My favorite outfit is 100 percent cotton and over four years old. I detest heels so much; I even opted for tennis shoes under my wedding gown. When I worked in the corporate world, I wore the same pair of black Mary Janes every day. Probably looked twelve, but that's okay. I've had to deal with red hair all my life; I'm used to looking like a child. I constantly get carded for wine. It's best not to fight it. Still, now that I'm home most of the time, poor David never sees me in anything but sweats. Although so far it hasn't affected his libido. I stare at him, thinking this, while he reaches for the phone. The wine is swirling in me, light and airy.

"Should we get some food?" he asks. "With the wine, I mean."

"I have a better idea," I say. I do this exaggerated wink to keep the theme going, which I'm sure is erotic and tantalizing as all get-out. David raises his eyebrows.

"Your temperature up today?"

I nod, my grin tempering the heat in my face. David unwinds his tie, drains his wine glass, and pulls me up. He kisses my nose, somehow making it sensual.

He's very gentle in the bedroom. For us, trying is never stressful. "You know what I'm thinking?" David says afterward, replacing his glasses.

"Mmmm…sausage and mushroom?" I prop up on an elbow and kiss his shoulder.

Just then the phone rings. It gives us both a start, although it is only 8:30 p.m. on a Wednesday. But wine and baby-making have a way of distorting time.

"Must be California," David says.

Something about taking a phone call from Alden while I'm naked just doesn't seem right. I hold up a finger as I hurry into my bathrobe. By then, David has answered. He's right. It's California, but it's not the brother I'm expecting.

Chapter 7

Alden

Not the most romantic way to start a first date, but Kiki worked until seven and our reservations at Sabina's are at 7:30, so. Here I am picking her up at the Mobil station.

Kiki acted all surprised when I asked her out, but I don't think she was. I can be very direct at times. She had to know I was scoping, hanging around when she rang up people's Twinkies and stuff.

Sabina's is only a few blocks from Mobil, so we walk together in a comfortable silence. That's a hard thing to do, be silent and comfortable at the same time. But we manage it. Only when I take her hand does it get a little awkward, like we don't fit together exactly right. But I'm willing to work with it if she is. Kiki's, like, super polite and thanks me profusely when I open the door for her. She's wearing this plum-colored shirt that falls off her shoulder a little, showing a white tank top beneath. Foxy, for sure. She's got that child-like quality that makes me feel like I'm robbing the cradle, but she's got a laugh that makes me want to giggle.

Everything's going peachy. Kiki's totally impressed when I tell her I've been volunteering at Rue Phillip's Oncology Clinic. But then when I tell her about my novel, *Allie*, she makes the connection. And then it all goes downhill.

"So, you're researching then? That's why you're volunteering?"

Now I feel like a phony. "No, I mean, yeah, I guess. Partly. But I am interested in helping others too." All of a sudden, I'm flailing. "My girlfriend, Teresa—I mean *ex*-girlfriend. She kind of…inspired me."

Way to go, Romeo. I should stop talking, I know it. But Kiki's looking at me like she wants to hear me. Like, she's *really* listening. I mean to change the subject, but instead it all spills out.

After three months of dating pretty hard, when we knew it was for real, Teresa showed me altruism. No joke. We were at Buddy Grady's pad after a Fourth of July parade in San Diego. We met this dude, Denton Howard, a big, jovial type who liked his beer and a good game of Euchre. He was the only dude in the bunch who had a kid, which was why we were at the parade to begin with, so his daughter (Ariel was her name) could see the floats and whatnot. The thing is, his daughter was a quadriplegic. Saddest thing you'd ever seen. It was a humid day, and everyone took turns cooling her off with a spray bottle. I wondered if Ariel even wanted her neck sprayed. But no one really knew, since she couldn't talk or move or anything. She just sat there and watched the action. I mean, I *think* she knew what was going down. But that's the thing. Here she was, a five-year-old girl stuck in a chair, and no one could tell if she dug the parade, no less getting water sprayed on her neck. It was a total downer. For real.

So when we got back to Buddy's pad, I looked the other way while Denton's wife took Ariel in the den and turned on some lame cartoon for her, set her up on the couch to give her a break from the goddam chair. We were all party-hardy, playing Euchre and drinking brews. Even Denton's wife was letting loose. I hate to admit it but I kind of forgot Ariel was even there.

You're probably wondering what the heck this has to do with Teresa. Here's the thing. At some point, I got up to grab another brew. Just past the fridge is the den, so I could see Ariel in there staring at the boob tube just like she was staring at the parade. Empty-like. It had gotten dark and the light flickered on her face kinda eerie and I just wanted to go back to my card game with the guys. Then a lamp clicked on in there and I heard a voice talking to Ariel. Not just any voice. Teresa's voice. *My* Teresa. My jaw kinda dropped and I stayed hidden by the fridge, my unopened brew freezing my hand.

"Did you like the parade, Ariel?"

No answer. Of course there was no answer. What was Teresa doing?

"What did you like best?" Then she went on, her voice all animated. "I liked the old-timey fire trucks. My favorite part was the bagpipes. Don't you just love the sound of bagpipes?"

I risked a peek and saw Teresa holding Ariel's feet, massaging them as she talked. Ariel's face stayed the same, but her eyes kinda came alive and she blinked a lot. It sounds corny, but I got choked up right there by the fridge. And I'm such a goddam pansy, I didn't even go in there. I hid in the can to chill and then went back to the card game. Never did talk to Teresa about it. I regret that, for sure. She didn't mention it either. That's the thing.

She didn't even care that no one noticed she was doing such an unbelievably nice thing. She was that good.

I never forgot that moment. Teresa did that to people. Inspired them. Now I want to do something like that—help a sick person feel human again. I'm not sure if I can do it, but I'll be damned if I don't try. I wish I had done it when Teresa and I were actually together. Then maybe she would've thought I was worth it.

Kiki listens with her forehead all scrunched. She's a kickass listener, I can tell. I know I should thank her or something, but I can't even look at her. What a pansy. Going on about how great his ex-girlfriend is on a first date? How lame.

But Kiki surprises me.

"Well, whatever the reason is, I think it's a really great thing you're doing. And Teresa sounds pretty great too."

"She is," I say, a lump forming in my throat.

There goes any chance of scoring with Kiki tonight.

That's okay, though. Something about the way our hands didn't fit together told me we're meant to be friends.

The rest of the dinner goes so well, I hate to admit it but I think we're both relieved. How long was she going to go on being polite about it? How long was I?

We go and see a movie after. *The Frisco Kid* with Gene Wilder. Good flick. It's a comedy but we're laughing at our own stuff, taking turns tossing popcorn and catching it in our mouths. Some dude in a red jacket comes over and scolds us: "You kids settle down."

You *kids*? That kills me. I like hanging with Kiki, though, especially if I get to act like a kid.

Chapter 8
Jerry

"You sound surprised to hear my voice."

"Surprised?" Fiona says. I can picture her shaking her head. "Jerry, I think I forgot what your voice sounded like. How are you? Is everything okay? Is it Alden? Did something happen?"

She sounds so much like our mother, I almost tear up. I clamp my jaw, irritated with her big-sistering; I could practically be her father. "No, nothing happened." I pause. For a moment I almost change my mind. Maybe this isn't the best idea.

"Jerry?"

"It's good news, actually. I…I've actually got a book deal."

"Oh, Jerry, how wonderful! Congratulations!"

"Well, hey. Don't get too excited just yet. The thing's gotta sell." Another pause. "Is this a good time to talk?"

A few beats pass, and I wonder if she gets it. There is no such thing as an easy silence between me and Fiona. But she was always intuitive, even as a kid. I wonder what she's intuiting now. *Good old Jerry, only calling when he wants something.* I start to heat up. Maybe my approach was too abrupt. I should've planned it out better. I could've written a script for myself. (I can always think better on paper.) But reason seems beyond me by now. I don't know what I'm doing. I take a deep breath and start over.

"I'd like to hire you, Fiona. To do the publicity for my book. The whole works. You know, after it launches and all that jazz."

"Oh! I see. You need interviews. A press release."

"Yeah, all that. Mitch is convinced all I need is some good press and they'll be knocking down my door again." I pause to let this sink in. There's no way she'd know that I've been out of work for almost a year, and hopefully I won't have to say it. I clear my throat. "Um…we also want to put together a book tour. I'll handle LA—but I need your help in Boston and New York. What do you think?"

Fiona actually sounds happy. "I think that'll be fun!"

"You do? Is that a yes? You'll do it?"

"Of course."

"Great! That's just…great."

"So, tell me about the book! What's the title? What's it about?"

Of course, she would ask. I *really* should have thought this through. "We're still finalizing the title. It won't be ready for several months. Maybe in the fall. I'll get you a galley then." She waits. "It's about…well, why don't you wait and read it yourself. That way you don't have my bias or anything swaying the message." I'm relieved—that actually makes sense, and I can tell she buys it. The receiver shakes in my hand. I've got to get off. "But hey, Alden doesn't know anything about it. So don't tell him. Don't tell him anything, okay?"

"So, it's a surprise for him too, then?" Her voice lilts, all innocent and happy, like we're talking about a visit from the Tooth Fairy.

"Yeah," I say. "Sure. Hey, I gotta go. I'll call you when I have more details, okay? Take care, Fiona." And I hang up.

It feels way too hot in here. Man, I'm glad I waited until Alden was out on that date before calling Fiona. I still feel like a gangster-type arranging people's lives like pieces on a checkerboard. But this is all for the greater good. I save my career, Alden gets his story out there, and Fiona gets to help the family. That can't be a mistake. Not to mention, maybe it will be a way to mend our relationship—mine and Fiona's.

I want to trust her. For this to work, I have to.

It's easier, I guess, that she has no idea how much she pissed me off. Or if she does, she's never given any indication. To her, we've just been acquaintance-siblings...for years. Before the review, and after the review. Business as usual.

I'd been writing for Hollywood for over a decade, moving up, paying my dues—from copyediting to drafting to plotting major scenes. Then I had an opportunity to be head writer for a new comedy called *The Boatnicks*. It was a fun movie about quirky misadventures at sea when the Coast Guard comes to the aid of pleasure cruisers. It was never meant to be heavy. It was the kind of movie you see on a rainy afternoon to give you a lift. Anyway, Fiona had graduated from BC with a major in Communications and Public Relations—and her first job was writing book and movie reviews for a local newspaper in a Boston suburb.

Yeah, you see where this is going?

So, she slammed *The Boatnicks*. Hated the film. Used words like "cliché" and "forgettable." Actually discouraged people from seeing it. To Fiona's credit, as I came to understand, she was a newbie at the paper and wanted to establish a name for herself. She wanted to be taken seriously, as she always had as a kid. She refused to be wooed by a fluffy comedy with a predictable, romantic subplot. I get that. But from my side, here was my kid sister dissing me *in print*. It was embarrassing. Insulting! If that weren't bad enough, the only reason I saw it is because *The Boston Globe*, for whatever reason, picked it up and ran it in the Arts section of the Sunday paper. Her review was all over New England. A buddy from the military mailed it to me, recognizing Fiona's name, not even realizing that I was the one she was trashing.

When I called her, furious, she apologized up and down, claiming she had "no idea" I had anything to do with the film, which I'm still not sure I believe. She offered to retract the review, but we all know nobody reads retractions. So I suggested she make up for it by writing me a stellar review on my next project.

Which has yet to happen.

The way I see it, Fiona owes me one. With this book. She really should do it free of charge.

But the whole thing, it's just too close to Alden. She's not dumb. Far from it. She'll know exactly where it came from. She's so patronizingly honest, she's probably incapable of keeping any secrets—much less one from her favorite brother.

Ah, what the hell. It's going to come out at some point. And if everything goes the way it's supposed to, by then everyone will be so happy about the book's success it won't matter.

Listen, I'm in the writing business. The biggest open secret, especially here in LA, is how many people ghostwrite. They write, and someone else gets the credit—but they get the money. Alden doesn't want to be famous. My name on something is worth more than his is. He's got to get that. Even Alden has to get that.

Yesterday, I gave back his journal. It was harder than I thought it'd be. I mean, there was no reason for me to hold onto it. I'd typed it all up. Not only did Mitch have a copy but so did our editor over at Little, Brown. There was no need for me to keep Alden's sloppy, hand-written version aside from the fact that giving it back made me feel like a royal shit—as if the act of handing it over implicated me in stealing it. I'd always planned on giving it back, figured I'd feel relieved to be able to give it back, or at the very least find something ceremonious about it. But I didn't.

All it did was remind me that it wasn't mine.

Alden was going through the mail when I got home, walked up to him, and set it on the table in his line of vision without a word.

"Ah, there she is," he said. "Sure it's in there?" He peeked under the flap. "Yup. About time, Jerr. What the fuck were you doing with it anyway?"

My lie was automatic, as was my fake laugh. "Damn, I kept forgetting to bring it home!"

He looked at me in that sideways way he had. Damn, I hated that. "Truth is, Alden," I said. "I wanted to finish reading it. And…it kind of spurred an idea. So I've been working on that." It felt good to say something that wasn't entirely untrue.

"Is that how it goes? That how things work in your world?"

I wasn't sure exactly what he meant, but I ran with it. "Well, sure! It's just like you being inspired by our little brother…"

"So, you're writing about me?" His eyes were questioning.

"No. No. No." I shook my head, a little too emphatically. But he kept looking at me with those eager, puppy-dog eyes. He's got the kind of eyes that are hard to lie to.

But somehow, I managed. "Absolutely not."

He nodded in this methodical way that told me he didn't completely believe me. Then he patted the black binder in a slightly creepy gesture of affection, and went back to the mail, leaving the binder right there on the table. I wished I'd just left it on his bed.

That inspiration—it's no joke. I've already insisted on printing a hearty acknowledgment to Alden as the inspiration. He *did* inspire this book. And it's not *exactly* his journal—I mean, it's been edited. And after the title and book cover and all that jazz, it won't have any resemblance to his handwritten pages in an old black binder. And all the names are changed…

Well, there was only one name I didn't change. Allie. I just couldn't do that.

I mean, *some* things are sacred.

Chapter 9
Alden

Volunteering is a pacifist's coping mechanism. I get things done for people, and I don't sock my older brother every day. Word. So far, they've had me file patient records and stock gowns. Boring stuff, but I believe in giving back. This is also research.

On my way out after my shift, I stop at Babs's desk at the volunteer station. I lean in all friendly.

"Hey sunshine," I say, as I do every day. Babs, volunteer coordinator here, must be about seventy-five. Her hair is so white it's like a cloud landed on her head. She smells like baby powder. No one dare mess with her when I'm around. Not if I can help it. She's like my grandma. About the nicest lady you'd ever want to meet, that Babs.

"Your shift over, Alden?" she says, trying not to smile.

"Yeah. Any word on when I can get to the third floor?"

Babs sighs with her whole body. "My dear Alden, *please*. Why you would want to set foot on pediatrics? It would just about break my heart to pieces. I like it down here at the front desk, managing volunteers. I don't even have to deal with patients. I can pretend we're all working at a hotel."

Babs doesn't need to know how much I'm dying to meet some patients. She'd want to send me to the funny farm. But that would make all the difference for my novel, *Allie*. Make it believable.

"They must need volunteers up there too. What about deliveries?" I ask, giving my best movie-star smile.

"You'd have to get a uniform." She pinches her lips around a pen and raises an eyebrow. Ol' Babs. What a gal. She must've been a fox in her prime. She writes something down. "I'll look into it for you, okay, dear?"

I would squeeze her right then. But she'd probably get spooked. Besides, it's against hospital policy, I think. So I tell her bye and split.

I suppose I could've told Babs the whole thing about Teresa, but I didn't want to get into the whole sob story. It would've been a huge downer. Not everyone is like Kiki.

What I decide to do is head to the HR department. I weave my way through the hubbub of the clinic, careful not to squeak my Adidas on the linoleum floor. I totally dig the energy of this hospital. Everyone's serious but generally in a decent mood. It's not too rushed or frantic; I could never volunteer in an ER, for crying out loud. Here, you can always find someone to share a cup of joe with. That's why I'm trying to get Kiki a job here. I think she would be happier than at that dirty Mobil station. Besides, it can't be that safe. Especially since I found out she sometimes works the midnight-to-seven shift.

Sylvia is the secretary in HR. She's got a personality like a bag of rocks. Nothing like ol' Babs. I fold my hands in front of me, kind of sheepish-like.

"Hi, Sylvia. I'm checking on the status of the data clerk position. Has it been filled?"

Sylvia doesn't look at me, even though I said her *name*. She just sticks her long, skinny nose in a folder and squints like she's trying to read something in Chinese. Then she puts the folder down. "No, it has not," she says, still not looking at me.

"For real? Okay," I say. Then I really snow her. "Sylvia, if you wouldn't mind, could you check on the status of Kyra Curran's résumé?"

Sylvia blinks like mad in my direction. Not exactly eye contact, but progress. "And you are?"

"A friend."

Sylvia straightens her back like she's up against a pole, and sticks out her miniscule pointy boobs. I swear this woman is a witch. "I cannot possibly keep status of all applicants. We've had over fifty. That would be a waste of my time."

I shouldn't snow a woman like this, but she's already cold as ice. "Of course you're busy. What a job you're doing. For real. I hope they appreciate you here. Thanks for your efforts, Sylvia. You've been an enormous help." I look at the carpet, and then make like I'm about to leave.

It must've worked. Sylvia wiggles in her chair. "What did you say the name was…of the applicant?"

"Kyra Curran."

"Just a moment please." Sylvia adjusts her cardigan that hangs impossibly on her thin shoulders and disappears into another room. She's gone a few minutes, and when she comes back, she's kinda smiling. I wouldn't have thought it was possible, folks. But there it is. And it's not a half-bad smile, either. It certainly helps her cause.

"Yes, Ms. Curran came in yesterday for an interview. From what I can tell she's still in the running. So to speak." Sylvia pats the top of Kiki's résumé back into a folder. "That's all I can tell you now."

Now I totally ham it up. "Wow, Sylvia. You are the *best*. Thank you so much!"

I start to split. But then Sylvia kinda calls out to me. "Mr. Donohue makes the final decision. The position should be filled by the end of the month. If you want to share that with your friend, I think that would be fine."

Movie-star smile again. "Thanks so much, Sylvia. I'll come back myself to check, and to visit. If that's cool."

Sylvia has color in her face and is trying really hard to suppress a smile. Women are so funny. It doesn't take much to figure them out, I kid you not.

It's this awesome, cool California afternoon outside. As soon as I turn on Hauruff, I toke my doobie. What I want to do is go straight to Mobil and tell Kiki the killer news, but I forgot when she said she'd be working again. I decide to stop home first and give her a ring. If she's not home, she's probably at Mobil. I need to check the mail anyway.

I don't pray as a rule, because as a rule I'm strictly spiritual and not at all religious, but I've been coming close to praying lately. About my book.

It only took about a month or so to type it all up. Jerry actually helped some. He told me this story about Allie's obsession with the alphabet that I had totally forgotten. Then he helped me craft a query letter. I had never even heard of such a thing before, but I guess all authors have to do it if they want to land an agent. What it is is kinda like a pitch. You sum up your book, give the 411 on your experience (which I totally lack), and that's basically it. It was wicked hard, though. Word. I had to read it to Fiona and rewrite it because she's the spin doc and all that. But geez, it was nerve-wracking to send those puppies out. Jerry says it's the bane of breaking into the publishing world, which I've learned is kinda like winning a freaking lottery. No one told me agents were so goddam picky. I started getting rejection form letters in the mail a few weeks ago. They trickle in like unwanted credit card applications. They all say the same, lame thing: "Thank you for your submission. Despite your interesting premise, I'm afraid this work is just not right for this agency." Blah blah blah. Then they add, "Remember, this decision is subjective and another agent might feel differently." Or some other baloney like that. Whatever. Another thing: most of these agents are in New York. So much for Jerry's contacts. He did give me a two-page list of agents though. That's the list I'm working from. I wait to get a rejection before sending another query out. Kinda keep the hope alive.

So I'm on my way home to check the mail. I don't have to tell you what I'm hoping to find. I have no idea what an acceptance letter would even look like.

I get to Jerry's pad and, instead of checking the mail right quick, I go inside to chill for a few minutes—to toke a little on the couch. I grab a Coke, too. Boob tube goes on nearly by itself. But I turn it off lickety-split because I want to be fresh. That tube can make you dumb if you're not careful. I swig my Coke and feel bubbles in my nose. I mean to relax but I end up pacing the goddam place, staring out at that lame view. Whatever. Time to get the goddam mail. I'm still standing at the box while I flip through. Aha! There's a letter for me. They spell my name wrong, but that's typical. I force myself to sit at the kitchen table and—breathe—before opening the envelope. My knee is going bananas, though, bouncing like mad. Another swig of Coke spits some fizz onto the envelope and I kinda panic. Rip it open. It takes me like four seconds to see it's another rejection form letter. "Despite your intriguing premise, this is not exactly a good fit for our list." Blah blah blah. I crumple the paper in my fist. I want to throw it at something, but instead I set it on the table and stare at it, as if it will tell me my next move. I'm all bummed now. I was so on top of the world just a few minutes ago. Now I don't even feel like going to find Kiki, I'm so down.

And now, of course, I'm thinking of Teresa. When is she ever going to get to see that I've done something? I pictured her seeing my name in block letters on the spine of a hardcover at B. Dalton or someplace. Don't get ideas—I'm not naïve enough to think she'd want me back. But it might convince her she didn't totally waste her time.

I'm still staring at the ball of paper, which slowly unfolds before my eyes, like a flower blooming, when the phone rings. I can reach from where I'm sitting so I answer it right quick.

"Jerry. Wow, you're home. Thought I'd get your answering machine. You shouldn't drive so fast."

You shouldn't talk so fast, I'm thinking. That blooming paper ball is, like, hypnotizing. That hit was probably bigger than I thought.

I start to tell the guy I'm not Jerry, but he talks over me.

"Listen, Jerry. We need to talk about the title. I'm not sure I'm loving *The Phony Rebel* anymore."

There's that tingling behind my eyes again, like I've been caught. Everything else kind of falls away and I'm pinned on his every word.

"It sounds too generic," he says. "Besides—and more importantly—Little, Brown isn't loving it. I told them it was tentative anyway but we won't have much time. Yeah, they're expecting galleys to be done sometime in August and launch in September. I need you to work on your publicity schedule. You gotta use your contacts in the Northeast because there isn't a budget for travel. But we gotta get you out there again. Then maybe we'll be able to get your name rolling on the credits like the old days. Fuck, I'm getting ahead of myself. Listen! Just get me, say, three or four legit titles tomorrow. We need options. We'll make our decision by noon. Got it?"

I kinda grunt, "Uh-huh."

"Good. But hey, you sound like shit, Jerry. Get something to drink, a good scotch maybe. See you tomorrow."

Click.

I'm still holding the goddam receiver when I hear Jerry come in.

Chapter 10
Jerry

I'm not usually home in the middle of the day and I'm banking on Alden being out volunteering at that cancer place. I'm just not in the mood to chitchat with him about Allie and his book, or Kiki, or his random revelations about spirituality. Or, most recently, his whining about agent rejections.

Like, the other day, he asked: "Why is it so hard to get an agent, Jerry?"

He had three rejection letters from three separate agencies spread before him on the table.

"I know, kid. It's tough for a first-time author. Heck, it's tough for a veteran author." I leaned on the back of a kitchen chair. "You know, I once heard of a guy who wallpapered his bedroom with all his rejection letters."

"Why would anyone do that?"

"I don't know. I guess he thought it was funny?"

"It's stupid. For sure a fire hazard."

I started laughing then. "Right on!" I was trying to speak his lingo, but I sounded like a buffoon. See, right then I wanted to tell him he was getting published. He *was* a good writer. All right—it pained me to say it, but it was damn true.

Everything is moving fast. I think we could be making a record in publishing history. Our publisher is even pushing the process. Randi, our editor, is adamant that over-editing our piece would damage the purity of the voice. So we've only gone through about four rounds, essentially grammatical changes. It's incredibly thrilling.

See, it feels too damn good. Everything's jiving for me again. Gosh, it's been so long. I deserve this, I really do.

But I'm not completely ignorant in our situation. I get that it's a shitty thing to do to anyone, no less my brother who's already had his share of problems in life. That's the funny thing about this whole business—you get addicted to the highs to get you through the lows. Sometimes, all I want to do is click my heels—and other times I want to pull the plug on the whole thing before he or anyone else finds out.

But I think it's too late for that.

As soon as I walk in I can tell he's home. First, the telltale reefer smell. Then, the mail all over the coffee table, the lamp on even though sun is pouring in through the bay window. I click it off before I even take off my shoes. Alden's in the kitchen. Oh well. If he's stoned at least he'll be in a decent mood. I take my time before saying hello, hit the bathroom first. I even slap on some extra aftershave.

But after I round the corner, I know something's up. Alden's face has that suspicious glaze to it. Damn! What now? He's got his hand on the phone receiver, like he's holding it in place on the wall. His eyes are slits and his mouth is open a little.

Then I see the rejection on the kitchen table, still recognizable in its half-crumpled state. So that's it. "Oh, no. Another one?" I try to sound sympathetic.

He nods slowly. "What's your agent's name again?"

"My agent? Mitch. He's been with me for years. Decades, actually. Why?"

Alden saunters into the living area and mumbles incoherently. Next thing you know, the Beatles are blasting from my boom box. That hard spot in my chest relaxes, but my shoulders tense. Even for Alden, this is strange.

I follow Alden into the living room. He ignores me. He's sitting on the couch like he's in a funk. I realize I'm angry. I mean, I am the veteran here and he needs to understand the proper order of things. I switch off the music and stand in front of him.

"Alden, why are you asking about Mitch? You know, you can't just piggyback on to my agent. Just because Mitch represents me doesn't mean he would automatically take on any projects of my brother's, or my sister's. I mean, hell. Even if Mom wrote *Great Expectations* from her grave, she'd still have to go through the query process like everyone else." I stop then; my words are sour in my mouth.

Alden just looks at me. "If Mom wrote from her grave?" he says finally, incredulous.

Jesus. I'm a total loser.

In the bathroom, I lock the door and run the sink. I just let it roll, full force.

In the mirror, I look the same, just an average-looking guy. I must have been the tester pancake in my family because it seems everyone but me (and my dad) was blessed with striking good looks. But I'm used to my face, washed out and unremarkable, and expect to find comfort in my reflection. All I feel is disgust. Even after washing my face and smoothing my remaining hair down, it's no use. My breath fogs the mirror. I shut off the light and stare at where my face looked back at me. In a bit I can see its contours again. I guess I'm stuck with it.

I venture out. Alden is exactly where I left him. "Alden, I—"

"He called tonight, your agent," he says, like he's just plain tired.

"Oh?" I clear my throat. "What did he say? Did he leave me a message?"

"He thought I was you," he says, and laughs coldly, with no mirth.

My mouth has dried up as if I just ran four miles. I stay quiet and in a minute, he goes on.

"He wants new titles."

"New titles?"

"Yeah, Jerry." He's all cocky now. His voice is animated. "*The Phony Rebel* isn't going to work after all. You need to come up with four new titles by tomorrow morning."

A bead of sweat rolls down my back. I hold my gaze steady, mentally bracing myself. But nothing happens. A few beats later, in fact, Alden seems almost normal. He even yawns without covering his mouth. I suddenly want to hug him. Instead, I say, slowly, "Oh, okay. Thanks for letting me know."

Back in the kitchen, I open two bottles of Budweiser, and bring one to Alden. I pick at the label on the bottle, wishing I'd never turned the music off. I'm peeling a corner of the label clear off the bottle when Alden says, "So, do you want to hear my suggestions?"

His suggestions?

He goes on. "It's been a while but that's probably cool. Like, I have perspective. So, my ideas might be pretty good. And it's not like it's my journal, *verbatim*, or anything. I mean, who would do that, right?"

"Right," I croak.

"It did take me by surprise, for real. But I can't lie and say I'm not a tad bit flattered."

"Flattered?" The earth seems to be rotating at lightning speed. I focus on my feet flat on the floor.

"Right on." Alden slurps his beer and sighs. "It's kinda cool my journal inspired you to write a book. And you're getting it out there lickety-split. You must've written it at the speed of light. Now I get why you're never home, brotha. You're in the grind, working so goddam hard." He laughs, sucks on his beer. I can't believe what I'm hearing.

"Have to admit, though," he adds. "I am kinda green about it."

"Oh?"

"For real! While I'm busting my ass just to get a goddam agent, you've *sold* a book." He scratches his scalp. Astonishingly, he's still grinning. "So, that's why...I don't think it would kill you to share him."

"Share...him?" My mouth is full of chalk.

"Word. Mitch!" Alden says, his voice rising in excitement. "I mean, at least make the intro, bro. Let him read my stuff. Can't hurt, right?"

"Right," I say, and manage to put the bottle to my lips to finish it off.

Chapter 11
Alden

She was right on, Babs. It's wicked sad on the third floor. Peed-Onk (that's what they call it). Sadder than anything. But it's good for me. Not only is it good research for my book, it kinda feels like penance. I mean, I wasn't around during Allie's decline and it's always irked me that I never got to say goodbye, like, officially. That's probably why I went zappy and broke all the goddam windows in the garage that night. Losing a brother sucks, totally sucks. But *knowing* you're going to lose him and not being able to say *goodbye*, tell him you love him and you'll miss him. That's the worst. Mom and Dad never apologized for that part. Probably felt like they were protecting me.

So there's this boy named Daniel Halsted. Seven years old and fighting some strain of leukemia—the good kind, they say. As if there could be such a thing. His parents both work because their bills are piling up like mad, so when he's in for treatment, he's mostly alone. They finally let me hang with him, once they got the skinny on me. I've been in here every day for the past three weeks. Daniel's a funny kid. Wiry but tough. Always clutching a baseball that's signed by Nolan Ryan. Not sure how his dad swung that one, but the kid loves that ball. He knows all kinds of stats too. More than I ever did. It always amazes me how kids get fixated on something and learn everything there is to know about it. If grown-ups could do that without getting so distracted all the time, imagine what we could accomplish?

Daniel's totally cool. It's bittersweet, though, because he's getting discharged today. I mean, I'm beyond psyched he's well enough to make a run for it, but I'm gonna miss the little dude.

I go in and he's sitting up watching the boob tube, spooning chocolate pudding into his mouth.

"What, you didn't save me any?"

Daniel's eyes light up. "Hey, man!" That kills me how he calls me *man*. "I'll just buzz the nurse and get some more."

"No, no. I just ate. I'm good."

We watch *Tom and Jerry* for a bit. He goes bananas for it. Loves it when Jerry outsmarts ol' Tom-cat. I put a pack of UNO cards on his side table, in case he wants to play. He likes playing cards with me because I never *let* him win like most people. The sympathy forfeit. But today he's cool with ol' Tom-cat getting his nose pinched.

"So, today you're out of Dodge, huh?" I say. "That's awesome."

"Yeah. Mom says she's going to buy a huge box of chocolate pudding at the supermarket. Says I can eat as much as I want when I get home too."

"Thank goodness. I would've had to smuggle some to your house."

Daniel nods, gets thoughtful. "You can come visit me at home sometime."

"Oh yeah?" I get up and do my Charlie Chaplin imitation for him. Cracks him up. Then I get an idea.

"Hey, maybe I can get your baseball schedule. I can come to one of your games."

That gets him quiet. "I don't know, Alden. I don't know if I'm going to be able to play."

"Really?" I say, shocked. "Why? You're better!"

This is where I'm a total doofus. Why do I have to go and say something so ignoramus? A nurse comes in with another thing of pudding. Daniel's parents come in right behind her—a whirlwind of love. I'm superfluous now. While his mom and dad *ooh* and *ahh* about getting him out of bed and into real clothes, I give him a thumbs-up and split. Makes me sad how I didn't really say goodbye. And the last thing I said to him was that lame thing. But it's all right, it's not about me. He's beyond psyched to go home. As he should be. What seven-year-old wants to be socked up in bed all the time? I think about Allie and his Legos. Poor kid.

Of course I hope Daniel doesn't make another appearance here, but I wonder if I'll ever see him again.

So now I want to revise *Allie*. Add the chocolate pudding and maybe even *Tom and Jerry*. Hopefully, I can get some edits in before that meeting with Mitch, if Jerry ever makes it happen for me. When I told Fiona about the Mitch connection the other day, she sounded surprised.

"What gives, Fiona?" I said. "Why are you shocked Jerry's hooking me up with his agent?"

"No, sweetie. No...I think it's great. I just thought...maybe Jerry was so busy with his own projects he might not have the time."

"Don't you think I should meet his agent? Don't you think *Allie* is good enough?"

"Oh, of course. It's absolutely good enough. And after your revisions based on your research, it will be even better."

I chewed my cheek a bit. "Fiona, do you think Allie used to eat lots of chocolate pudding in the hospital?"

A big sigh. "Mom would know."

"Maybe I should call Dad and ask him?"

That made us both crack up.

It doesn't matter, though. In my book, Allie's going to eat all the chocolate pudding he wants. Clean out the hospital stash. Get direct shipment from Jell-O. I'll make sure he has a never-ending supply. Word.

Chapter 12
Fiona

I'm sitting at a window table in Ruthie's Café waiting for Teresa. I'm shamefully early, but I was eager for the excuse to come downtown and immerse myself in the energy of my favorite city. It's been some time since we've seen each other, Teresa and I. My best girlfriend, my BC roomie…I can picture her now, leaning over her oceanography textbook in her cat-eye readers, her topknot unraveling, highlighting nearly every line of text. "Everything's important!" she'd say with a throaty laugh. Never would I have thought someday in our lives weeks would pass without our seeing each other.

Today, though, she's asked me to lunch. I can guess as to why, and my heart hurts for my brother. Alden and I talk nearly every day and somehow, as if by unspoken agreement, Teresa never comes up. Sometimes I'm afraid I'll slip, especially with the news she'll probably share today. Oh well. Just one more thing to keep from Alden. I'm still not sure what to make of Jerry's insistence that Alden not find out about his book, whatever it's called. He never even told me. It's just so odd. I mean, Alden's writing a book too. He'd surely cheer his brother on. Maybe it's dedicated to Alden? Ah, that's probably it— Jerry plans to put Alden's name front and center in italics on the dedication page. What else could it be?

I'm smiling about how that dedication might read when Ruthie's front door flies open.

Teresa walks in, flushed from the spring wind that seems gustier on Newbury Street. She unwraps her scarf as she hugs my shoulders, insisting I stay seated. She looks beautiful. Healthy. Happy.

I sip my iced tea and wait for the announcement, for her ring is nearly blinding with sparkle, but I don't want to spoil her news. She asks me how I am, about David, my freelance work. We chat about current events. But even as we trade sighs over the Mount St. Helens tragedy, and the elderly man who refused to leave home, wanting to die with his volcano, his lifetime companion—I can feel my brother's heart breaking three thousand miles away.

No one was more surprised to see them get together than I was. Teresa is lovely, but she's often overlooked. Not like Linda, who attracts attention like a beacon, with her flawless complexion and her perfectly styled hair. Teresa's best quality is found inside, and that's what most people miss. Hers is the most generous heart, but it takes a special person to understand it. Which is why, when I thought about it, Alden must have been drawn to her. He's always been sensitive, despite his "cool dude" act. I loved them together and was so rooting for them to make it. I even visited them in San Diego once. They took me to the zoo, and it was like I was teleported back to my childhood. We got slushies and cotton candy, laughed at the monkey picking his nose, rode the carousel at Balboa Park. We even got our faces painted from a sidewalk vendor. It was silly and wonderful. Teresa and Alden held hands the whole day, snuck kisses when they thought I wasn't looking.

They were together for over two years. It filled me with joy to see him so happy. I kept expecting an announcement, but not the kind that eventually came. I'd never seen Alden cry that way. He never did tell me what happened exactly. I'm not sure he knows himself.

Now, at Ruthie's, I raise my eyebrows with a grin, prompting Teresa to blush and look at her hands.

"It's true," she says, fondling her ring. "Chad proposed. We're getting married!"

We stand and embrace, our hips bumping the table adjacent to ours. I say all the usual things: how happy I am for her, how gorgeous her ring is, how great she looks. It's all true. But when our sandwiches come I dare to mention the elephant in the room.

"So when do I get to meet the lucky guy?" I fight to keep my tone light, because I can't believe I have to ask this question. Before my wedding, Teresa would practically have me scan potential dates for her. Now she's engaged and I haven't even met her fiancé. I'm sure it has everything to do with Alden, but still. She was my friend first.

"Oh, Fiona. I know. You really need to meet him. You would love him. He's smart and funny and devoted. He's got this great sense of adventure. We've talked about doing the Peace Corps together. Or—can you imagine an African Safari honeymoon?" She grins and bites into her club sandwich.

"I've always loved that about you, Teresa. You're fearless, always up for an adventure."

I mean it as a compliment, of course. Perhaps subconsciously, I was recalling that she and Alden had trekked cross-country together. But Teresa stops chewing. I think she might cry, but then the waitress is there checking to make sure everything is to our liking.

When we're alone again, Teresa clears her throat. "You know, Fiona, I never wanted my relationship with Alden to become a wedge in our friendship."

My face gets hot and I know I'm as red as my hair, but I shrug casually. "No, it won't. Don't worry about that."

Teresa looks at me intently. "You haven't met Chad yet."

"Well, everyone's busy."

"Not too busy to keep the love of my life from my best friend."

Love of her life? What was Alden then? My mouth gets so rigid I cannot take another bite of my sandwich. But I force composure. "Well then, we'll just have to change that."

"Yes! And soon. Because there's something else."

Something else? I wrap a hand around my glass of iced tea, craving the cold, working to keep my face neutral.

"Chad and I won't be going on safari for our honeymoon, as it turns out. And there's a reason we got engaged after only six months. Don't get me wrong, we knew we were meant to be right away, but we didn't feel it necessary to get married unless, until…" Her voice trails off.

"You're pregnant," I whisper.

Teresa nods, then smiles. With the light coming in I see her laugh lines crinkle in celebration. We're on our feet hugging again, our hips bumping the same neighboring table. As we embrace, I look out the window. There's a woman pushing a stroller right there on the sidewalk. Mothers are everywhere.

"Congratulations," I say.

Although Teresa asks me to join her for a walk along the Esplanade, I decline and head back to Lexington. But a solo walk sounds like a cure so I hit the Minuteman Trail near my house. I barely get a hundred yards before the tears start.

This is good. I managed not to cry in front of Teresa, and I'll get it all out of my system so I won't burden David again. I've been crying all too often lately and my poor husband doesn't know what to do with me.

My best friend is bubbling over with joy, and I'm happy for her, but it's a distant kind of happy, because I know how much Alden loved her, still loves her. Should I keep this from him? I don't know. Maybe I should be straight with him. Tell him right away. He should know. Poor Alden.

And then there's the envy—unkind, perhaps, but true. How could I not be envious? She didn't even intend to get pregnant and—oops! It's so unfair.

But even worse than that is our friendship, or what it has become. Nothing is the same, and it won't be, ever. This is the saddest realization of all. The grief is almost too deep for tears.

I get back to my car at a good clip, sober and congested and in need of a nap. Thank goodness I'm just a few blocks from home.

Our house is warm and smells like cinnamon, cheering me slightly. I have at least three hours before David gets home. It takes two hours to get early pregnancy test results. Why not try one? Maybe that's why I'm extra emotional. I hurry and organize the vial and test tube onto the stable bathroom counter. After adding my urine, I blow my nose and brush my teeth. I brush out my hair that's snarled from the wind. It gets all frizzy and big and I mat it back down with my headband so it doesn't tickle my face.

That was the only thing Mom and I used to fight about: my hair. Allie and I (and even Alden a bit) inherited Grandpa Eddie's bright red hair. Mom, whose own hair was a mousy brown, let Allie's grow into an unruly mane of red spirals when he was three—*a la* cowardly lion, pre-makeover. But me—she always wanted to mess with mine, contain it in pigtails or barrettes or, worse yet, braids. But then Allie got sick.

I never blamed Mom for being gone so much. When Alden was home from boarding school, he made us Hamburger Helper. We ate it in cereal bowls on the floor watching *Little Rascals*. If there were any Hostess cakes in the pantry, Alden would let me have two. He let me stay up late, taught me how to play gin rummy. But when Alden was away at school, which was most of the time, Dad would warm me up a TV dinner with a phone to his ear. He'd sit me in front of *Howdy Doody* and duck into the home office for the rest of the night. Which left me alone a lot.

I missed my mom. When she did come home, I wanted to be next to her every moment. If she happened to be awake before I left for school, I let her do whatever she wanted with my hair with no fuss. I'd force a smile in hopes she'd catch it in the mirror. But one morning she did a curious thing.

She started out fine, brushing my hair and parting it down the middle. Then I watched her hold a handful of it, my hair, and stare at it for the longest time. She must've forgotten I could see her in the mirror because she didn't try to hide her crying like she usually did. Tears streamed down her cheeks and she started sniffing, as if using a tissue would give her away. She tried to keep her mouth closed, but then her lips parted and she let out a wretched wail, cutting through the dead quiet of the bathroom and bouncing unapologetically off the tiles. I didn't know what to do, so I kept very still and waited. I thought she would finish my hair, but she did another curious thing. She bent down and put her face in it, kind of smelled it. Her tears wet the part in my hair. Then she patted it as if it were the fur of a household pet and left the bathroom without a word. I looked at my reflection for a while after, thinking she might come back to finish. But she never did. My hair fell naturally to my shoulders in messy, uncombed curls—just how I liked it. But it made me so sad. I tried to do pigtails myself just to make her happy. They were crooked, but I wore them to school anyway.

I found out as I ate my cereal the next morning—Dad mentioned it over his newspaper—that Allie was losing his hair at the hospital. He said it as if it were a known thing, as if I should have been expecting it. I had a hard time swallowing my cornflakes after he said that. I had never heard of anyone losing his hair and it scared me silly. I had nightmares for weeks. I kept pulling on my own hair to see if it would come out too. It never did.

I felt awkward around Mom after that. I hooked my hair into baseball hats. I wrapped it like Aunt Jemima when I did my homework. If it were hidden, maybe she wouldn't be so sad. But it didn't seem to matter. She'd come home from the hospital, her bloodshot eyes looking at nothing but the floor. And then on the day Allie died, it was like another person came home. Her still-bloodshot eyes were now unfocused and empty, as if a zombie invaded her body. She had to take pills to help her sleep. In the mornings I would wait at her door, peering into the darkened room for any sign of stirring, and then again in the afternoon. She often slept all day long. When she wasn't sleeping, she wailed and called for Allie, which sent a flash of terror down my spine. I hid under my covers, wishing she'd just go back to sleep. She was never the same after Allie died, but she was still my mom. And I loved her more than anything.

My heart is heavy as I click off the bathroom light-switch. I wallow in the darkness for a moment, allowing myself time to feel pain. I wrap myself in my favorite afghan and curl up on the couch. I mean to read the newspaper, but my tears have made me sleepy. I doze off in no time. My internal clock is astute, however. I awake exactly at the two-hour mark.

My whole body tenses as I return to the bathroom to check the test tube, then deflates. Negative. I squint at the tiny mirror at the bottom of the test tube and see a warped reflection of my hair. My heart sinks into my knees. Why is this so difficult? We are doing everything right! What I wouldn't give to find a positive result on that stupid test. It's supposed to be over 90 percent accurate. I wonder, is this the kind of test Teresa used? When her positive result took her by surprise, did she cry tears of joy or was she fearful?

I can picture her rushing into Chad's arms, kissing him, confessing her love for him before breaking the news. Of course, he was thrilled. He should've been! He'd secured a future with the best woman on the planet. Maybe he proposed right then. Or maybe they talked about getting married in a very unromantic, logical way: "In the best interest of the child..." Who knows? I don't even know the guy. I can only hope he's deserving of such grand luck.

This afternoon, oddly, it's not my disappointing test results that make me cry. It's the thought of this stranger, this man who will marry my best friend and be the father of her child, whom I wouldn't recognize on the street if I saw him.

Chapter 13
Alden

Kiki and I are meeting for lunch today at Tangy Mango. We arranged this three days ago, and I remembered! For real, I would forget my own birthday if Fiona didn't call first thing. I kid you not.

After lunch I think I'll swing by and confab with Babs, even though I'm not volunteering today. The Tangy Mango is totally nearby. Besides, I don't see Babs so much anymore because now I'm always on the third floor.

At one of the window tables at Tangy Mango, Kiki's grinning so hard I think she might explode. She's kinda drumming the table with her fingertips, and when I get closer she busts out: "I got the job!"

We high-five, and she holds on and shakes my hand in the air. Her curls bounce around and it's like she can't stop smiling. I've never seen her so excited. It's adorable. Almost makes me want to scope on her again.

"They said they would give me two weeks but if possible, start next Monday," she says. "I already told Mobil. Steve didn't even care, I don't think."

"Sure he did. You're sunshine in that place."

We order avocado burgers. That's another thing I like about Kiki: She's not afraid to eat a decent burger. If I sit through another dinner with a chick eating a salad, I will sock somebody. Kiki orders french fries too. Awesome.

She uses half a bottle of ketchup after all is said and done. Totally rad.

"You'll dig working with Babs," I say.

Kiki shakes her head. "No, I'm working with Sylvia."

"Jump back!" I slam the table.

"She's training me." Kiki grins and then slurps a slice of avocado. "So, how's it going with the book?" she asks. She's the only person I've told about *Allie* besides Jerry and Fiona.

My turn with stellar news. "Aces. Jerry's setting up a meeting with his agent and me. I think he's going to look at my stuff."

"That's so cool!" she says. "But what do you mean 'you think'? What else would he do with your stuff?"

"Right on. But to have a *meeting*…"

"That's good, right?"

"Word. But, I dunno. This isn't the norm. Usually you query, then they ask for a sample, then maybe the whole shebang. *Then* they ask for a meeting. Or a phone call. This is happening ass-backwards."

"Well, that's why you have your brother. This is how he's helping you. Consider yourself lucky you don't have to go through all that stuff."

She's got a point. I wash my burger down with Coke. Without waiting for the bill, I put down plenty of moolah to cover our burgers and a decent tip. I totally get a bang out of that. It's an awesome thing, not having to worry about money. Thanks, Grandma Gallagher.

"That's all she wrote," I say. "Let's walk."

Kiki's in such a groovy mood, she's up for anything.

Except, apparently, going to the clinic to meet Babs.

"I just think it's bad luck to go there before I've started working. Especially to socialize."

It's a bummer, but I get over it right quick. I'm not one to harp on one little tweak in my day. Instead, we walk to my pad. Kiki wants to see what a rejection letter looks like, even though I've told her what they say, like, verbatim. All three thousand of them. Ha! I'm laughing about it, at least.

"That's not so bad," she says, holding twin rejections from separate agencies.

"That's the whole point! It would be better if they were like, 'Get a clue! You can't write worth donkey balls!'"

Kiki's cracking up, crinkling the letters in her lap as she doubles over.

"Right on. Let's destroy them," I say. I rip one letter to shreds, grunting like I'm wrestling a wild animal. I use my lighter on the other one, making a torch. Kiki thinks I'm hilarious. I toss it in the kitchen sink and run water over it before the fire alarm is set off.

Afterwards, I offer Kiki a glass of water because I know she doesn't drink Coke. But then I'm not sure what to do with her. She starts wandering around our pad, paying no attention to the lame view.

"Is this your brother?" She's found a picture Jerry dug out of his closet the other night. It's from years ago, during one of our summers in Maine. He's leaning against the rail of the porch steps and I'm straddling a tricycle; one of my chubby legs is in midair. I like that picture, even though I don't remember that time. Allie was just a baby. Fiona wasn't even born yet.

Kiki's smiling kinda sad-like, gazing at it.

"Do you have any brothers or sisters?" I ask. I should already know this, but we've never talked about her family.

"I have a younger sister," she says flatly. "She's exactly four months younger than me."

I don't have to be a biology wizard to know this is impossible. I screw up my eyebrows at her, and she laughs. "My parents finally got pregnant, after years of trying. But they had already filled out the paperwork for me and I guess they felt bad backing out."

I feel like a half-wit. "Come again?"

"I'm adopted." She puts down the picture. "For a long time it was just…weird. My sister and I don't look anything alike. Not even close. People would always stare. I grew to be, like, two heads taller than her. She's a skinny little thing. Blonde, fair. Lives in New York now. Trying to be an actress or model, I think. Kristin. That's her name."

Kiki sounds so sad. And I can't think of something cool to say, so I kinda put my arm around her. She squeezes my hip and moves away.

"I know my childhood would've been so different had she not been born," she says. "Is that terrible to say?"

"No."

"I mean, there would've been room for me. Our family Christmas pictures would have me front and center between my parents, instead of lurking behind my dad like an interloper."

Now she is looking out at our lame view, but I can tell she doesn't totally see it. I want to hug her again but I don't think she's into it.

.

"But the thing is," she goes on, "I love Kristin more than anything in this world. I doubt she even knows it."

I get my doobie ready. What Kiki needs is a nice toke. "Why not go to New York then?" I say. "What keeps you in LA?"

"Distance. We both needed it," she says, and smiles a little. "We're very…different. We barely even talk anymore."

I'm out to lunch. But considering this is girl stuff, I'm not surprised. "Why not?" I hand her the doobie.

She shrugs and takes a mini-toke. I bring it in deep. On the exhale, Kiki changes the subject. "Tell me about *your* sister."

"Fiona!" I say. "Only my favorite person ever! But I have a better idea. You've got to *meet* her."

Fiona's line picks up after three rings. I hear laughter before "hello." Fiona has company. My smile fades as my jaw gets heavy. The voice on the other end is no one I expected.

Teresa.

I stammer out a hello and ask for Fiona. But before she puts her on, I can't help myself.

"Teresa?" I say. "What are you doing at Fiona's?"

"Well, hello stranger. Fiona and I are going through some baby catalogues. Getting a registry together for the shower."

"Shower? *Baby* shower? Who's having a…"

I sink onto the couch, light-headed. Kiki sits next to me, but I can't even look at her. I'm transfixed on the boob tube's black screen just because it's in my line of vision. Fiona's in the background asking who it is. When Teresa says my name, there's a battle for the phone.

Fiona is there now, her voice low. "I'm so sorry, Alden. I meant to tell you. I didn't want you to find out like this."

My mouth is hanging open. When I try to speak, nothing comes out.

Now Teresa's voice is in the background: "Wait…he didn't know? You didn't tell him?"

"I guess there are some things we need to catch up on." Fiona tries to be aloof, but sounds panicky.

Next thing I know, the receiver's out of my grip. Kiki's taken control. What a pal. I sit there like a goddam vegetable.

"Is this Alden's sister? This is his friend, Kiki. What's going on over there?"

Kiki's quiet for a long time, listening to my sister relay the whole sob story. Please, Fiona, do me a solid. Don't make me look like a doofus in front of Teresa. Kiki's got this serious look on her face, and then she turns away, saying "Uh-huh" and all that baloney. I feel so empty right now. Depressed as hell.

"Well, tell her congratulations," Kiki says, in her best monotone. Then she hangs up. She's staring at the carpet when she says in this apologetic tone, "That ex-girlfriend of yours, Teresa? She's engaged."

I hold up my hand. I've had enough. I don't want to hear it. I don't want to know the guy's name or where he works or how firm his handshake is. I don't want any of it. Kiki has the sense to figure this out.

She stands, smacks a kiss on my forehead, and sees herself out. It's quiet after she's gone. Graveyard quiet. I would normally be blasting some Beatles at this point, but I stay put on the couch, letting it all sink in. Something happened on that phone call. In just a few minutes, my world totally changed. I feel it in my whole body. It's not just in that one spot; I don't know why they call it heartache.

Of course, the earth is still turning. Right? The sun will rise tomorrow. It will happen. Right? Somehow I'm still here, another dude trying to figure it out. It seems impossible, though. It totally does.

The phone rings. It, like, pierces my eardrum. I don't want to answer it, but it keeps going. I finally pick up, then wish I hadn't.

"Hey," Jerry says. "Listen, get your manuscript and get over here ASAP. Mitch has an opening this afternoon. We should nab it. Can you be here in an hour?"

Chapter 14
Jerry

Alden comes into the office looking like he just rolled out of bed. Really, brother? I don't say anything—I don't need a scene—but I do try to give him a look. I introduce him to Nancy. Normally, he would immediately start charming a pretty girl like Nancy but today he barely looks at her. He seems distracted, but not in the usual annoying Alden way. It's almost like he's...sad.

Shit. He knows about the journal. Jesus, that would be the way it happens—just when I've begun my penance in bringing him to Mitch. It couldn't have been Fiona; she doesn't have the galley yet. Did he see something in the office? Is the manuscript lying around somewhere for anyone to see? I'm scanning Nancy's desk for any incriminating evidence when the office door flies open and in comes Mitch like a hurricane thrust. He's got a wrapped sub under his arm and a bulging folder in his hands. He doesn't look in the mood for an impromptu meeting. Nancy shoots me a look.

"Mitch!" I sort of stand in his wake. "This is my brother, Alden."

To anyone who doesn't know Mitch, he appears to be friendly and welcoming. He shakes Alden's hand and says "Nice to meet you" and all that. Only Nancy and I can tell how irritated he is.

"Hey-ya. Did we have a meeting?" he says and juggles his load to show us his sandwich. "I was going to go through some slush while I eat my lunch."

"Yeah, go ahead. Eat. This won't take long. Alden has a sample of his book for you."

Another millisecond of annoyance, and then we're all in Mitch's office. He sighs, unrolls his sub from wax paper, and starts eating.

I look at Alden. *Do something.* I discreetly serve up the moment with a wave of my hand. After Mitch's third bite, Alden finally starts talking.

"Thanks for meeting with me," he says, giving his stoner smile. "I'm not sure how this works. I've never met with an agent before."

Why did he have to go and say that? Mitch rolls his wrist: *Get on with it.* His sub is nearly halfway gone. This man does everything like he's in a race.

I jump in. "My brother's written an excellent book. Commercial Fiction, I think it would be. Alden, tell Mitch what it's about."

Alden clears his throat. "Well, it's kinda autobiographical. Not totally. I mean, *I'm* not that fascinating. But it's about my—I mean *our*—younger brother Allie. He died when he was eleven. Leukemia."

Alden pauses. Mitch doesn't react, just keeps chewing. His lips are all greasy.

"But it's not a total downer," Alden says. "It's kinda got a fantastical element to it. Mystical, I like to say. Do you get me? It's not that Allie has superpowers, but he kind of knows things. And helps people. Kind of like a guardian angel." Alden straightens in his chair. "Word—I just thought of that. Yeah, he's like a guardian angel."

Mitch is wiggling his fingers over his sub in lieu of using a napkin. His eyes dart from Alden to me, back and forth. I'd like to hope he's considering Alden's novel, but I know better. I just hope he's not too ticked at me.

"So," I say quietly. "I guess it would be Adult Fantasy."

"No, no," Alden says. "I would almost say it's nonfiction. But it isn't. I mean, Allie was a real kid. Right? But I had to make a lot of stuff up. But however you want to sell it, Mitch."

I squirm inside. Mitch gives me a crooked smile. He finds a brown napkin under the wax paper and wipes his mouth.

"You need to nail down your genre," he says. "You've been querying, Alden?"

"Yes! Yes, I have."

"Why don't you leave your query letter with Nancy and we'll take it from there?" Mitch says.

Alden chuckles, his voice hoarse, and at that moment I realize he's *high*. Jesus, Alden. You freaking burnout! You couldn't hold off until tonight?

Alden scratches his scalp, and props an ankle on his knee. "I didn't bring my query with me today. Just my manny. Didn't think I needed it. I mean, we're already having a meeting, you know?"

Mitch doesn't say anything. I can tell he's pissed, but he's being polite. "That's true," he says. "I don't usually meet with authors face-to-face until I've signed them on." He glares at me. I'm toast. "But considering you're

Jerry's brother, why don't you leave your manuscript in the slush over there and we'll see what happens." Mitch points to the wall behind us, which is lined almost to the ceiling with multiple stacks of paper.

Alden turns and his smile disappears. "Whoa! Look at that. That's not all—"

"Yup," Mitch presents it with wide arms. "This is your competition. Authors just like you who want to get agented."

Alden looks confused. I can't believe how naïve he is. Did he really think it was going to be easy? It's like he has zero respect for the publishing process.

But Mitch glares at *me*. "Leave it in the slush. And I'm going to have to see you out. I'm swamped, as you can see."

Alden looks at me; the disappointment in his face is palpable. I shouldn't have called him in today. This was a total mistake.

We start to go, but then Mitch is talking to me: "Oh, and Jerry, I spoke with Randi and the latest edits will be here by the end of today. Should be the last. And it looks like that issue with the galleys got squared away, so they'll be on time. So line up your publicity calendar and get things moving, okay?"

"Sure. No problem." I'll have to call Fiona later today. She's lining up interviews in Boston already. Then I think we're hitting New York. I'm working it around in my mind as I leave, too excited to notice that Alden is lingering in Mitch's office. I'm halfway out the door when I hear him say, "So, what title did you guys decide on?"

I hurry back into the office, grab Alden's elbow. "That's okay. I'll tell you all about it at home. Let's boogie. Mitch is busy." I'm talking as fast as Mitch now.

But Mitch leans back, his hands cradled behind his head. "Oh, you're one of the privileged few who have seen this fucking masterpiece?" He waves his hand toward me, as if announcing a king. Maybe he isn't so pissed after all. Still, I pull at Alden to get him out of there before—

"For sure," Alden says, grinning. "Well, not the final thing Jerry came up with. But it was my journal that inspired him."

Mitch's eyebrows nearly hit the roof.

Alden keeps at it. "I'm sure it's smart as hell. I gave him an idea for a title. But which did you choose? I'm wondering if mine made the cut."

Alden is oblivious to the realization sweeping across Mitch's face. Mitch glances at me, suspicion in his eyes, and holds his gaze as he says, "Tell me, Alden. Which was your suggestion?"

Alden wags a finger and says, "No, no, no. You first." He's having a grand time. Playing games. Jesus, why did I call him in here? This was not supposed to happen.

"Go ahead, Jerry," Mitch says to me. "Tell him. I'm surprised he doesn't already know, considering he's the"—the word comes out like it's a virus—"*source*."

I should've taken off my jacket. My pits are a mess. "*No Phony Business*."

Alden nods thoughtfully, rubs his chin. "Huh? Oh. Got it. It's a pun. Okay. Kind of catchy. I guess it'll work."

"Your turn," Mitch says.

"I think the gist should be, like, you know that scene when I get the lyrics wrong and imagine all the little kids running through the rye patch...but the patch is on this cliff? So, in an ideal world someone or something would be there to catch them so they don't get hurt."

"Interesting," Mitch says, his voice as level as a lake on a windless day.

It would be better if Mitch would look at me now, so I knew what he was thinking—if he is pissed or whatever. But he doesn't. He just nods away, not taking his eyes off Alden. He's figured it all out, I'm sure of it. This is worse than if Alden found out. Mitch could call the whole thing off and my career would irrevocably be in the toilet. Now I'm really panicking. Shit.

Shit. Shit. Shit.

"What are you calling *your* novel, Alden?" Mitch asks.

"*Allie*," Alden says with a shrug. They share a smile. I feel invisible.

They say their goodbyes while I back out of the office, avoiding Nancy's I-told-you-so look. She doesn't know how right she is, but for a different reason. Alden catches up to me and I whisper, "Let's get out of here."

"Hey-ya, Jerry. Hold up!"

I make my way back to Mitch slow as a snail. I would never believe I could tremble, but here I am. Like I'm made of pure caffeine. Why did I let Alden come in here? This could be the end of me. Way worse than the *M*A*S*H* fiasco. *Way* worse.

Chapter 15
Fiona

"What do you think he's going to be like?"

I squeeze David's hand three times over the console. He brings mine to his lips; his words are warm on my fingers. "I'm sure he's a good person. Let's keep an open mind."

We're on our way to Teresa and Chad's place for the big reveal. I had suggested we keep it easy and meet at a sports bar to watch the Red Sox, but Teresa insisted. "Chad loves to cook!" she'd said. As if I'll even be able to eat.

"Are you going to be okay?" David asks as he pulls off the Mass Pike. We're just a few blocks away from their newly rented house in Newtonville.

"Sure. It's about time I meet him, don't you think? If it hadn't been so long. I mean, my expectations surely have become over-the-top by now."

"Teresa wouldn't choose anyone less than wonderful, right?"

"Right. And this is the man Teresa chose over my brother."

"You have to give him a chance. See him for who he is. What would Teresa think if she knew how you felt?"

I gaze out the window. Alden is just half of it. "I think she knows how I feel."

We pull into their driveway and I double-check the address I jotted on an index card. The outside lights are on, but it looks like no one's home. "They're not home," I say, hoping it's true.

David smiles at the ground as he helps me out of the car, smart to avoid my eyes. I'm about to insist he drive me home when Teresa appears, holding open the screen door.

"Well, if it isn't my favorite couple," she says, beaming.

Teresa is one of those women who glow from the moment of conception. She's wearing an adorable peasant top that nearly conceals her belly bulge. Her arms are bare and slender. She's wearing makeup and turquoise beads. I quickly scan my friend and find, to my horror, her feet are in platforms. She actually skips down the driveway to meet us. She pinches my cheek affectionately, and plants a kiss on David's. She wedges herself between us, hooking arms as if we're walking down the yellow brick road, and leads us to her fiancé.

Chad meets us in the foyer, sporting a black-and-white checkered apron and holding a spatula. He's good at first impressions. Extremely handsome, he smiles broadly and locks his brown eyes on mine as he gives my hand a vigorous shake. He slaps David on the back and invites him into the kitchen. He looks athletic, clean-cut. Someone my mother would've picked out of a yearbook for me.

"I brought your favorite," I say, handing Teresa a bottle of High-Rise chardonnay.

Teresa taps her stomach with her fingertips. "Maybe I can have just one."

Whoops. I hide my ignorance with a grin. "Or I can just drink it all."

She plants me on the cream-colored couch next to the blank television, which should be showing the Red Sox game. But there is dinner music playing: instrumental with lots of saxophone. David and I can watch the highlights when we get home, I guess.

Teresa returns with two glasses of chardonnay. "Cheers!"

And the night begins. We are separated as if we are at a junior high snowball dance: boys on one side, girls on the other. The guys laugh in the kitchen over the sizzle of a wok. Teresa slides off her platforms and curls up on the couch around her slight belly bulge, petting it like a cat. I nibble on cheese to give my hands something to do while she talks about the baby.

"I know you're not supposed to say, but I think it's a girl!" She giggles behind her hand, as if we're in this together.

"Oh?" I gulp my wine. I just might polish off the whole bottle.

"Did you hear about Linda's new job?" Teresa says, and quickly adds: "Oh, right. I forgot. You helped her get the job. Didn't you do some freelance PR work for them too?"

Another gulp. "Not exactly. Should we put the game on?"

But then Chad calls, "Dinner!"

Teresa struggles to hoist herself from her seat. Instinctively, I offer to help her up off the couch. When she takes my hand, she doesn't let go. We enter the candlelit dining room holding hands like schoolgirls.

"Oh my," I say, eyeing the huge skillet of stir-fry that acts as a centerpiece. "I could get used to having my meals cooked for me." I sit on David's left and tickle his ribs.

"Thai peanut chicken," Chad says, setting his napkin on his lap. "Dig in!"

Everyone is focused on the food except me. It's too early for comfortable silences. I try to think of a topic to introduce with Chad, but nothing comes to mind.

"So," Chad finally says. "How did you girls meet?"

Ah, this I am happy to answer. I set down my wine and am about to tell him about the funny shoe mix-up in the locker room at BC when he says, "You know, I'm so happy Teresa has found a new girlfriend. It's just like they say. It gets harder as you get older to make friends, meet a buddy."

My words are lost as my mouth hangs open. Teresa must swallow her noodles whole. "No, sweetie," she says. "I told you, Fiona and I are friends from college. We went to BC together."

I try to smile, though judging from the heat in my hands, I'm sure my face is red. Friends from college? That is how she is describing our friendship? That could be Ursula, our RA, who recently organized a reunion of sorts. That's not me. Us. We were *best friends*. Gorging on pizza in the middle of the night, walking to class and calling it exercising, finding time for ice cream during midterms, sneaking laundry into the next dorm because the dryer was hotter, comparing crushes on that cute history professor, talking until all hours of the night about everything except schoolwork—because it was impossible not to talk, to share our every thought with each other. *That* was our friendship. Not just "friends from college."

I can safely assume Chad knows nothing about my brother.

David squeezes my knee three times under the table. He comes to my rescue once again. "Where did you go to school, Chad?"

The night continues in this fashion, a Chad McGovern show. I keep my eyes on my plate, unable to look at Teresa—although she's laughing, and chiming in when Chad tells the proposal story. I catch bits and pieces, but I don't really care to hear about how they met and fell in love and became engaged. And I realize as I stare at my empty wine glass, I don't even care about Chad. I don't. He could be the Republican opponent to Jimmy Carter and I still wouldn't care. I excuse myself for the bathroom.

I linger in the bathroom, just to have time to think. Teresa has a vanilla candle lit on top of the toilet. Somehow I'm comforted by this. In the mirror, I'm the same girl that was once best friends with Teresa, who knew—knows—vanilla is her favorite.

I open her medicine cabinet for no other reason than to see if there's anything I recognize. She's always loved Max Factor, and I'm sure I'll find it. But no. There's Elizabeth Arden all over the place. It's silly how much I feel like crying. She probably has no idea what's in my makeup drawer.

I return to a refilled wineglass, and I'm thankful. I drink, and talk as little as possible. But when Teresa pauses in her dissertation about pregnancy to promote my résumé, it seems forced and I have to stop her.

"It's nothing," I say. "I have a few projects, that's all. Keeps my hand in."

"Tell them about your brother's book," David says. I can feel Teresa tensing across the table. Oh, David. He must know I won't be able to resist this.

"I'm helping my brother with a publicity calendar for his book tour. His book launches in September and I have interviews lined up. Book signings too. We're going to New York the first week of December. I can't wait to see the windows." I smile to David at this last bit. He asked for it.

"Wait," Teresa says, her wine glass stopped in mid-air. "Your brother...published a *book*?"

"Yes! It should do very well. It's highly anticipated in literary circles. His agent and publisher feel this will do great things for his career."

David nudges me, but I ignore him. The frozen awe on Teresa's face is priceless.

"Yes," David chimes in, his integrity usurping my small victory. "Fiona's brother, Jerry, is a screenwriter, as you know. In the past he's only written for movies. But this is his first novel."

The night was over after that. We helped them clear the table and Chad invited us to stay to watch Red Sox highlights, but we were ready to leave.

"Why did you have to say anything?" I whine to David in the car.

"Hon, you don't want to deceive," David says. "Besides, she'd find out in a few months anyway."

"Maybe, maybe not." But I know he's right.

The Beatles are playing on the radio. *Hey Jude*. It seems to fit the mood, and from this moment forward I will always think of Teresa when I hear that song. David and I hold hands over the console again.

"I'm glad it's over," I say.

"Me too."

Remember to let her into your heart
Then you can start to make it better.

"Teresa looks good," I say. "Pregnancy suits her."

David hums affirmation, squeezing my hand.

"I hope it happens soon for us," I say, pressing on my uterus as if to call it to attention.

"It will," David whispers. "Don't worry."

At home, I nearly trip over a package in the darkness of our front stoop. I know immediately what it is, and my heart quickens. Jerry's book! I try to pry it open right there in the foyer. But it's got three or four layers of shipping tape, so David gets scissors.

"What is it?" he asks.

"You'll see."

It's quite an ordeal to open, and I'm out of breath either from the effort or excitement. David's at my side with a glass of water, telling me to sit. But I can't sit. I was sleepy in the car but now I'm wide awake. I have something special in my hands. I can feel its energy. I'm beaming at it, as if both my brothers are right here.

"Is that what I think it is?" David asks.

"Jerry's book. Advanced Reader Copy," I whisper. I'm so proud of my family, to have these amazing brothers who love and respect each other. I'm so glad Jerry asked me to be part of this, and feel as though this book is a ticket to his heart—that stubborn heart that never really let me in. I'm so grateful.

The cover art is abstract and appears to be a carousel horse. Intriguing. How I used to love the carousel! I quickly flip to its dedication, sure to find Alden's name there.

Instead I read: *To my mother.*

Now I do sit and I do take a sip of water. David turns on the floor lamp and I start at the beginning. I didn't expect to start tonight, but I can't help but read.

It takes less than a page to figure it out, but I read another few to be sure. When I slam the book shut, I'm breathless. My hand shakes holding the water glass.

"What time is it in California?" I ask David.

"Close to eight. Why?"

"I have to call Alden."

Chapter 16
Alden

"There's a request for your services on the third floor," Babs says when I check in on Monday.

"Bam! Even doctors can't resist the Gallagher charm," I say, totally out to lunch.

"No, Alden. This request is from a patient. He knows you." Babs tilts her head sympathetically. Her eyes are wet. I split before she can ask me anything.

The elevator ride takes a lifetime. I'm kinda holding my breath. I know what I will find on Peed-Onk. I just don't know how bad it will be.

Daniel's back. He hasn't been in for over four months. I had written him off like I'd never see him again. Hoping I wouldn't. But he's got something else now. Everyone's being all secretive about it. But I heard it's related to his treatments for the past two years. That kills me. For real. Medicine is supposed to heal, not hurt. All those goddam chemicals being pumped through him, making him weak and vomity and bald. They might take the cancer away but give him something else that could kill him. It makes me want to sock somebody in the jaw, even if I am a pacifist.

I knock before walking in because he would want me to. I'm glad I do because he puts on this, like, big smile for me even though he doesn't feel like it. I can tell. He's all hooked up and anchored on the bed. He looks so small.

"How's my favorite cancer patient?" I say, my standard greeting for him. He doesn't laugh today.

"Good," he says, but he looks green.

"Yo Danny, want some chocolate pudding? I'll get the nurses to bring us double, just like old times."

"I don't feel like eating." His voice is soft and scratchy.

"Want to play some UNO?"

"Makes me dizzy to sit up."

I do my Charlie Chaplin impression and get him laughing. But it seems like it hurts him, so I stop.

"Want me to see if I can find *Tom and Jerry*?" I ask. "I bet they're on. Or maybe *Scooby Doo*?"

He stares up at the small television but doesn't answer.

"Do you want to just rest?"

He nods. Goddam, he looks like hell.

"Maybe I can come back later?"

He nods again. His eyes disappear into these sunken, dark craters before I even leave the goddam room.

"Later alligator," I say, even if he can't hear me.

I nearly collide with his parents in the doorway. We've met before, but I'm surprised to see them here in the middle of the day. Mrs. Halsted says hello, but she's all out of it. Her eyes are raw and she keeps rubbing her hands together, spacing out. Mr. Halsted shakes my hand and gives me this intent look, which disappears when he blinks. He looks totally wiped out, like he hasn't slept in a decade. But they are super polite to me, considering what's happening to their son. You'd think this would make them just a little bitter. I would've given them a pass if they started throwing things.

"I was going to come back later?" I say, kinda asking permission.

Mrs. Halsted stares past me. Mr. Halsted takes my shoulder and leans in. There's coffee on his breath. "Thanks for keeping our boy company while we couldn't. We're not going anywhere this time. We both took leaves from work." He points to a big maroon suitcase propped in the corner. There's this awful heavy in the room. I say "good luck," which is probably not the keenest advice, considering. I'm such a goon! Mr. Halsted pushes the door closed. There's this loud, final clunk—as if to conclude my whole friendship with Daniel. Then I split. Have to. I'm kinda shaking walking to the elevator.

Never felt motion sickness on an elevator before now. What am I even doing? This is not about research. This is not about Allie—my brother or my book. This is about Daniel. My eyes fill up. Why does this have to happen to kids? Goddam, just let him grow up. Let him run, use his legs. Let him laugh and cry and fall in love. Let him become a father, a teacher, a coach. Let him live, for crying out loud. That should be a rule of God. No death until middle age. At least. Tears are really flowing now and I feel like I might puke. I keep picturing Daniel pointing at *Tom and Jerry* on the boob tube, with this open-mouthed belly laugh. The kind of laugh that adults are incapable of. I wonder if he'll ever laugh like that again. It hits me, a wave of panic. Will he ever laugh like that again?

I can't do this anymore. Going to tell Babs my volunteering days are over. I'm not cut out for it. For real. I'm the dude who hides behind the fridge when the better person rubs the feet of a five-year-old quadriplegic. I've had to let Teresa go, and I think I have to let this go too. I'll find another way to give back to the world. What good does a Chaplin impression or an UNO game do anyway? Daniel needs what Allie needed: a miracle.

I go to the can to calm down. Throw some water on my face.

I have an urge to call Fiona, even though I haven't talked to her since that fake-me-out phone call. All I want right now is love. Sounds corny, but there's no room for anger or pain. Life is too short. Anyone who doesn't live for love and peace just doesn't get it. That's it. I'm going to call Fiona as soon as I get home. Right after I see Kiki. Because—word—this whole thing with Daniel makes me want to see her too.

"Hi Kiki," I say, kinda sad-like, when I find her on the second floor. "Daniel's back."

"Really? Oh no." She holds her heart and gives me a sad face. She's solid, too, even though she's never met Daniel.

"He doesn't look so good," I say, picking up her mug of ballpoint pens.

Pens remind me of that game Allie and I used to play: Pick-up Sticks. I have an urge to dump them all on the floor and challenge Kiki. For sure I would win. I don't, though. For one thing, Kiki is not cool with sitting on any floor, like, ever. And another thing, Sylvia has already started in with the ol' hairy eyeball. I guess my charm has worn off.

"Oh, that's awful," Kiki says. "Did you go to see him?"

I tell Kiki about Daniel's parents.

"That's good," she says, sorrow in her eyes. "Any kid would want his parents there more than anything."

She's got a point. But I'm still going to miss that little dude. I would've liked to help.

Man, I have to get out of here. "Tangy Mango for lunch today?"

Kiki is squinting at her manual. She's got a stack of files in front of her that could rival Mitch's slush. Something tells me she's a wee bit behind.

"I brought my lunch today," she says.

Sigh. I tell her I miss hanging. Sylvia huffs. Kiki says, "I'll call you later." And it's like I'm pushed out the door.

Babs can't even go to lunch with me. She's got a hair appointment. For real, that woman always has a hair appointment. She's always terrifically coiffed. I tell Babs about Daniel and she tears up right there. I give her a big hug that leaves me smelling like baby powder.

What a downer day. The weather is even bogue. There's this misty rain in the air—too light for an umbrella but enough to soak you after a few blocks. Even my smoke doesn't like it. I puff right quick before it gets mushy. My clothes are drenched by the time I walk into Jerry's pad. And I'm cold. I ignore the phone ringing and peel off my clothes. I get the shower steaming, hop in and sway there, letting the heat pour over me. Word. I could fall asleep standing up right now. I stay in for ages. Then I stay in the steam, wipe a big circle in the mirror, and shave. The phone starts ringing again. I ignore it. It's not like I'm not going to rush around like a maniac just to answer the phone when it's probably not even for me. But by the time I'm dressed, the goddam phone's giving this, like, angry ring. Like it's had enough. It finally dawns on me that something might be wrong. Daniel? No way. His parents don't even know my phone number. I should give it to them.

I sprint to answer it now.

"Where have you been?" Fiona asks. "I called last night too. Alden, we need to talk."

"Yo sis, I don't give a hoot about that thing with Teresa. For real. I should apologize—"

"This is not about Teresa!" Fiona sounds impatient. This is a first. "It's about the book!"

"The book? *My* book? *Allie?*"

"No, not your book. Jerry's book."

"Oh. Right on." I wait. She sounds kind of panicky.

"Alden, you know I've arranged his publicity tour? It starts the first week of December, in Boston."

"I think Jerry mentioned it." He didn't, but…whatever.

"Well, you need to be on it."

"On…?"

"The tour! You need to be with him for all of it. Every interview, every book signing. Every bit of it."

"Why?"

Fiona sighs into the receiver. "I don't really want to tell you over the phone."

"Well, I don't want to wait until I get to Boston. Tell me why I need to be on that tour."

Then Fiona—*Fiona*—starts yelling. "It's not Jerry's words! It's *yours*, all yours. From when you were a kid. From after Pencey."

"No-ho-ho," I say. "I know all about Jerry's book. I met his agent and everything!"

"It's your *journal*, Alden. Your report from that clinic."

"No, Fiona. It's not...my journal. He just got ideas from it. Like, it inspired his story."

"Oh, yeah? What's the story?"

Good question. I have no idea what his storyline is. But it can't be. It's not...my journal isn't... gimme a break!

She tries about three different ways to give me the 411, but I still don't copy. Finally she says, "Listen, do whatever you have to do to get your hands on one of his galleys, you know, an Advanced Reader Copy. Read it for yourself. Then you'll see."

"All right." This whole conversation is giving me a bad feeling. Jerry wouldn't do something like that. Would he? I feel that tingling behind my eyes again.

"Just promise me you'll be on that plane with Jerry."

Chapter 17
Jerry

"He's sleeping," I tell Fiona, assuming she's called for Alden.

The phone woke me up out of a dead sleep. My eyes aren't cooperating yet. I squint at my alarm clock, which reads 4:53 a.m. This is out of character for Fiona, who has always been conscious of the time difference when she calls Alden.

"Actually, I was hoping to catch you." Her voice seems projected, like she's on stage. I hold the phone away from my ear, which isn't awake yet either. "Let Alden sleep," she says, "so we can get down to it."

My eyes pop open. "What do you mean?"

"I got your galley."

"Okay. What'd you think?" This might be a stupid question, but I'm still half asleep.

"What did I think? What kind of question is that? Did you really think I wouldn't notice? It's plagiarism, Jerry!"

"Now, now, little sis. Let's not start throwing darts here."

"It's nothing undeserved, *big brother*," she mocks. "It's an unthinkable thing to do. Especially to one of your flesh and blood! Is nothing sacred in your world?"

It's like she's speaking in rhymes. I have to take a second to wrap my mind around her words. "Well, hey. Let me explain—"

"Oh, please do. I would love to hear you try to explain yourself."

"Technically, it's not his journal anymore. It's been edited. And the names have been changed. And…it's been edited…by several different people…" I'm flailing, and she knows it.

"Oh my God!" Fiona yells. "None of that matters! It's still plagiarism! Jeepers, Jerry. You call yourself a writer? Do you have any ethics at all?"

"Fiona, just hold up. Relax. I don't need a lecture from you of all people."

"What's that supposed to mean?"

"I mean, you kind of owe me one here."

A beat goes by and then Fiona takes in a sharp breath. "Are you talking about my review? You can't possibly be talking about an article I wrote nearly ten years ago. Tell me you're not bringing that up right now."

"It was a shitty thing for you to do, Fiona. You took the film completely out of context, with no regard that your own brother wrote the thing—was head writer for the film. You slammed it!"

Fiona exhales loudly. "I don't know what this has to do with the issue at hand. Jerry, how many times do I need to apologize? You obviously have never forgiven me. Maybe no apology is enough—"

"You're right." I'm wide awake now. I'm perched on the edge of the bed, ready to bolt. My heart races with anger. "You owe me this, Fiona. I finally have something that can really make it. You need to make amends—"

"Oh my God. I need to make amends? Have you lost your mind?"

"I'm completely serious."

"That's what worries me," she says. She's quiet for a long time. We both are. I hear her sigh into the phone.

The sun is creeping up; a faint light fights through my cheap, plastic blinds, and I turn away, face the wall. I usually sleep through this part of the day. Seeing the sun rise always makes me think of what could have been.

Janine's face is right there. She's tilting her head at me like she used to do when I would surprise her with dinner from her favorite Mexican place or empty the dishwasher without being asked. Since the day I met Janine, I pledged to build my own family—ours, the right way. I thought I was doing the right thing. But I know now, a pedestal makes for a hard fall. Or you become scared, like a statue. So I fucked that up too, just like I seem to have always done with Alden and Fiona, never mind my dad. But at least I *chose* Janine. My siblings don't deserve special treatment just because we happen to be related.

And what of that, anyway? Since when have they even felt like family to me? A stoner brother and a duplicitous sister. Always looking out for each other, even now. I was the one who grew up and joined the military and went overseas while they soaked up all our family's money, lived high on the hog. I ate slop in a mess hall while they dined at the freaking country club. And Alden blew his tuition for private school. How much money did our parents waste on him? While I slept in a bunk! And Fiona. Little Miss Perfect. Can't do anything wrong, even when she's ruining her oldest brother's career. Screw them. Alden was right when he sent me away from the clinic that day. I've always been better off without them.

Fiona must be able to tell I'm crying. Her tone shifts. "Jerry?" Fiona says, much more gently. "You okay?"

Mom. I don't know how, but there she is, in Fiona's voice, like she's there, like I'm hearing her for real. My attempt at words comes out as a sob. Fiona is respectfully quiet, waiting for me to pull myself together, probably. I blow my nose and try to control my hiccup-y breathing.

"Jerry, talk to me," she says. "Please. I care about you. I'm your sister."

I should hang up on her. Just hang up. But I can't just hang up, be exactly what she expects. Not anymore. I'll say good-bye. Polite. Civil.

"Jerry. Please."

I hear myself talking.

"The truth is…see, I was reading it in the apartment and Alden seemed so bothered by it. So I took it with me when I went to my agent's office. I didn't mean for Mitch to get ahold of it. I just took it there to *read* it. But then, damn Fiona, it'd been so long since I felt like I was worth anything. I mean, years…"

"Jerry," Fiona says quietly. "I know the divorce was rough on you. I'm sorry about that."

I pause, seeing suddenly what my life must look like from the outside. To them. There's no way they would know about the *M*A*S*H* fiasco. They only see Janine, and heartache, and I can't bear to even contemplate that, not now, and certainly not from my baby sister.

I go on. "Anyway, Mitch thought it could be a hit. He took it, sold it…"

"And he thought you wrote it?" Her voice softens. "He still thinks you wrote it, doesn't he?"

"Yes," I say, relieved to finally admit it aloud. "I know it was wrong. *Is* wrong. But, honestly, Fiona? There's nothing I can do about it now. It's out of my hands."

A big sigh. "Well, not completely. You still can make things right."

The sun is fully up now, breaking through my cheap plastic blinds like laser beams. "What do you mean?"

"First off, be honest with him. And yourself. And Jerry, you need to apologize. Not just in words, either. You need to show Alden how sorry you are."

I have no idea what that would look like. "Fiona, that's not—"

"It's something you'll figure out," Fiona says briskly. "There will be plenty of opportunities on the tour."

The tour?

Oh no. Alden's coming with me.

Chapter 18
Alden

Why the hell they call it a galley is beyond me.

Not sure what's the buzz but Fiona sounded so freaked, I'm all over it. Screw asking Jerry. I'm going right to the source.

"Hey Nancy." I give her my movie-star grin, but I'm not in the mood for scoping, so I push on to Mitch's office.

"Wait a minute, sir," she says, stumbling out of her roller chair to follow me. "Sir, I'm sorry but you can't just go in there without an appointment—"

"It's okay. He knows me." *You know me too*, I want to say. Funny how she keeps calling me *sir*. Kinda cracking me up.

"Sir!"

As I open the door to Mitch's office, Nancy goes to grab my shirt. For real? Chill, sunshine.

But when I see Mitch, I kinda get it. He's deep into something. It's like his office is made of stacks of paper. There are white towers everywhere. Some in binders, some just punched together in a block. Like pillars holding up the room's Chi. He's hunched over a thick stack like he's trying to decode legalese. I would laugh but Nancy stiffens up so much beside me, the Chi starts buggin'.

It's like slow motion, the way Mitch lifts his gaze, which flickers to Nancy. Glaring. He blinks a little, waiting. Nancy starts *um*-ing and stuttering and dancing around like she's gotta whiz. So, I save her. Casanova that I am.

"Mitch, yo. Sorry to bug ya but I was in the neighborhood and thought I'd drop by."

He blinks at me now. For real? He doesn't remember me? It's not like I'm an average-looking dude. Word. Look at my bushy red hair.

"It's Alden Gallagher? Jerry's brother?"

He sinks back in his chair, chews his cheek like he's trying to solve a riddle. "Oh, right. The inspiration."

"Um, yeah," I say. "So, whaddaya say I get my hands on one of those galleys? Or one of those Advanced Reader Copies or whatever you call 'em?"

Mitch just stares at me, chewing his cheek.

"Do you have an extra copy floating around?"

Mitch waves Nancy away and kinda smacks his lips. The door closes behind me. Suspiciously secretive, whatever this is.

"Listen," he says, leaning over his reading stack. "I don't know what the fuck is going on between you and your brother. And I don't know—nor do I want to know—what his book has to do with it. But his book better *not* have anything to do with it. Do you hear what I'm saying?"

I hold back my confused squint. "Right on," I say evenly. "I copy."

"What's with this 'I copy' bullshit? Fuck, you seventeen or something? Grow up, kid."

"Love me or leave me," I say, grinning.

His eyes are daggers as he points his pen at me. "Let me be straight. Don't make me go Godfather on your ass." He almost spits, I kid you not.

A horse's head in my bed sheets. Far out, right? I chuckle a little, but Mitch's lips are a straight line.

"Or your brother's ass," he says, and adds under his breath: "I have plenty reasons to kick his right to the curb."

He clenches his jaw the way Dad used to when he'd get mad. Something went down between Jerry and his agent. I'm starting to feel like a dick going to him and not Jerry.

"Go and ask your brother for a galley," Mitch says. "And get the hell out of my office. And don't even think of coming back here without an appointment."

Chapter 19
Jerry

The Jeffersons is on—one of Janine's favorites. We'd curl up on the couch with bowls of ice cream and laugh at George and Weezy.

"Why can't you write for this show?" she asked once.

"Can't always choose what show you write for," I'd said. "And you never know what's going to be a hit."

It's turned up really loud to drown everything else out so I can pretend Janine is here. I even have a bowl of mint chip in my lap.

Then Alden barges in and starts rambling—I can't hear either him or the TV, they're both so loud. He steps between me and the TV screen, and I finally catch what he's saying.

"Mitch told me I should ask you for a galley," he shouts.

"A what?"

Alden reaches behind him and turns the volume dial way down. "A galley. Advance Reader Copy...whatever you call it."

I look at him steadily. "Why would you want a galley, Alden?"

"Why not?"

That innocent stoner look of his makes me crazy.

"Alden, they're not toys. They're printed that way for a reason. It's a marketing tool. We send them to reviewers to get the buzz going, not hand them out free to friends and family."

"Who's 'we'? You and Mitch?"

"Well, Mitch doesn't do the marketing piece. Or publicity."

"So, who is?"

"Well, sometimes it's the publisher. Or an independent publicist."

"Like Fiona?"

Jesus, she told him. Why would she do that? After I confessed everything, opened up to her. I told her to keep it on the down-low, from Alden especially. Had she already told him when she called me? Oh, damn you, Fiona! But I can hardly be surprised, can I? She's way too close to Alden to keep anything from him. Those two have always been, like, cosmically linked. "So what?" I snap. "So I hired our sister! Better than a stranger doing it."

"So what?" he repeats. "So give me a goddam copy of the book, Jerry."

"No, Alden. They're all out." I go to the kitchen, but he follows. "I don't have a bunch of copies sitting around collecting dust."

"But for sure you have at least one."

"Alden, give it a break." Why can't we wait for the tour and let Fiona smooth it all out? I wish I could stall him somehow.

"Why, Jerr? What do you have to hide?" He's leaning on the back of a kitchen chair, squinting like he's some big detective. I've come to the kitchen under the guise of refilling my ice cream, but I just toss the bowl into the sink and look for a beer instead. We're out. Of course. Alden's crossing his arms now, like he knows he's got me.

Fine. I give up. It's not like I can delay the inevitable forever now, can I? He's already gone to Mitch. There's a mess I will have to mop. Fiona probably has a copy of the book in the mail to him already.

"Fine," I repeat, out loud. Walk of shame to my bedroom to dig out my copy from under my mattress. The hallway back to the living area goes for miles. I'm torn between wanting to sprint or crawl my way back to my brother. But that victorious look in his eyes pisses me right off, so I toss it at him. "Here you go."

The relief as it leaves my hands is unexpected. I feel thirty pounds lighter. Hell, what is it anymore anyway? It's not his journal, not anymore. And I can't call it my book. I mean, once the process started and Mitch and Randi and whoever else combed through the damn thing, it doesn't really belong to anybody. It's just there.

I stare at the silent TV. George and Weezy aren't even in this scene. In a few minutes, the credits start rolling, so I click it off. It's so quiet I can only hear Alden's breathing and his turning of pages. I wait for what's coming.

"What the fuck is this, Jerr?"

I don't say anything. I assume it's a rhetorical question.

"What the hell's wrong with you?" he says, his face twisted like he smells rotten trout. He slaps the book shut and I wonder if he's going to throw it at me. But no, he just pounds on the cover and yells, "You ripped off my journal and published it behind my back? And look at this: 'by JD Gallagher.' Is that my name? Don't think so! What the hell? You didn't *write this*!"

"I know, Alden. But wait…" I reach for the book, meaning to show him the acknowledgments. "I give you credit—"

"Jump back! For real." He jabs a finger at my chest. "Stay away from me. Or I will sock you one, I kid you not."

I do as I'm told, more out of shock than anything. I sink into the uncomfortable-as-hell butterfly chair that Janine left me with. Alden fixes me with a glare, and then goes back to reading, flipping around to different sections the way Mitch did.

My head feels heavy. I'm such a phony. Funny how I can talk myself into anything these days. Of course it's still his journal. Doesn't matter how many people comb through it. It's his life. And he knows it. I die a little bit with each page he turns, the pain on his face stinging me. When he finally makes his way to the acknowledgments at the back, I hold my breath. He's got to be somewhat gratified when he sees—

"I'm your *inspiration*? That's supposed to make everything cool?"

Okay, not gratified. I rub my throbbing forehead. I think of what Fiona said: Tell him the truth. Apologize.

"No. It doesn't make up for it," I say, the words thick on my tongue.

"Like hell it doesn't. You totally faked me out! You *stole* my journal!" He paces the room, his fury radiating like heat. I can't bear to look at him. "You played it off like it was yours."

He slams the book against the wall, making a mark on the paint. "How doggish! And—goddam—I think it's *illegal*."

"It is," I say, because it is.

"I'm gonna sue your ass. Fucking yellow, pansy-ass bastard!"

His face swells with anger, growing more red than I've ever seen it. He charges me with the book held high, as if to club me with it. I go to block with my forearm, but he stops just in time and gets in my face.

His whispered words send a chill down my spine. "You are a cheat. You have less integrity than a raccoon that steals other people's stinking trash and eats it."

He backs away from me. "You are not my brother," he says. "Not anymore."

Chapter 20
Fiona

The phone startles me awake. Of course, it's Alden. I grab the receiver and shut myself in the bathroom so as not to wake David.

"Did you get a galley?" I ask, my throat full of frogs. "Did you see it?"

"What a royal dickweed," Alden says, and I can't help but grin. He goes on: "That's not why I called, though. Yo, I made some edits for *Allie*. Important edits. Essential. Was thinking you need the latest."

"Oh…right. I would love to read your new version. But with all the planning for the tour, I'm not sure how much time I'll have."

"Word. About the tour. Was thinking we could promote *Allie*."

My head is foggy from sleep. "*Allie*? But you don't have a publisher yet. You can't promote an unpublished book. It hasn't even been edited. You don't want to generate excitement about a book not yet on the market."

Alden makes a humming noise. He's not going to let this go easily, I can tell.

"Alden, did you talk to Jerry? After you read it, did you guys talk about it?"

"Not much to talk about, sis."

"Well, I don't know about that. Jerry seems to be in rough shape. Maybe this whole thing is a cry for help—"

"Jump back, Fiona. For real. Dude is not getting any sympathy from me."

"I know. It's inexcusable what he's done, but he's our brother—"

"No. He's not my brother anymore. I've disowned the cheese-weasel."

"Oh, Alden—"

"Word. I'm gonna split then. It's late for you. Go hit the hay."

Click.

As if I could get back to sleep. Of course, I cannot blame Alden for his anger. But Jerry—I could feel his anguish. What he did was awful, but it wasn't premeditated. It grew into something out of his control. I have to help Alden see that. We are family. Families need to stick together, no matter what.

I don't bother getting back into bed, but instead tiptoe downstairs to visit the fridge. Mom would always say, "Milk soothes you to sleep." Well, there's milk in ice cream.

Tonight, it's Rocky Road. I dig my spoon right into the carton. The only light in the kitchen comes from the moon—pitching like a sail through the bay window. When my eyes adjust, the backyard is awash in a soft, white light, making the world feel like a silent, mystical fairyland. The large oak stands authoritatively at the back of the yard, a watchful, sturdy guardian, its turning leaves a sober reminder of time passing. There's a wide swath of flat grass just before it—the perfect spot for a play-yard, I've always thought.

I drop my spoon. Suddenly, that's it. I will not be able to bear living in this huge house through another holiday without hope for a family of my own.

I took another pregnancy test tonight, before bed, but for the first time, I don't even want to check the results. Why chase heartache, again and again, like the moonlight over our barren yard?

And I know from heartache.

You know when you walk by a storefront window and catch your reflection in the glass and for a moment you don't recognize yourself? And you have to think: Wow, this is how other people see me? Yesterday, I finished Jerry's book/Alden's journal. I read about his little sister as if she weren't me…this little girl I thought I knew.

I was ten years old, in fourth grade. Ms. Fitz was my teacher, the one who licked chalk off her fingers. My desk was in the second row next to Elaine Carver, who liked to pick her nose. I remember these little details so vividly, but I can't picture myself.

After the principal's secretary had given me Alden's note about hitchhiking out west, there was no question what I would do. I ducked out of school during lunch period and ran home fast as the wind. The only suitcase I could find was one with a big sticker that read "Whooton"—the other private school Alden dropped out of.

What does a ten-year-old girl pack to run away from home with her big brother?

The standard: a couple dresses, underwear, socks. I tucked my notebooks half-filled with Hazle Weatherfield stories in the front pocket. Aside from the notebooks, I had two other essential, precious things: the moccasins Alden helped me buy a few years before, and his red hunting hat. That goofy hat! With oversized earflaps, it was like a blankie for your head. I loved that thing because Alden gave it to me. I had no idea before reading his journal what it meant to *him*, though. Rather than pack it, I wore it to meet him. It was huge on me and kept falling over my eyes, but if I propped my hair under it just so, it stayed put.

I snuck down the back stairs and dragged that old Whooton suitcase all the way to the Museum of Art. He met me as I marched across Fifth Avenue, puffing up my roller-skate-skinny body with each proud step.

But Alden was not keen on my accompanying him on his grand runaway scheme. Of course he wasn't! What sixteen-year-old boy would want his ten-year-old sister tagging along? But I didn't see it that way. He kept insisting I go back to school, which was the most ironic and confusing thing. Here was the consummate high school dropout lecturing me on how important school was. But of course, all I heard was that he didn't want me around. That broke my little-girl heart.

Who knows why he decided to take me to the zoo at that moment? But at the time I didn't care. I bounded onto the carousel platform to find the perfect horse. I liked the realistic-looking horses, even though I knew it was a ride and the horse was plaster and all. The idea of getting on a purple horse made me feel like I was Dorothy about to get tricked out of her dream. I chose this big brown horse with chipped paint and a missing ear. And when the old-timey music started and the lights blinked, I giggled with the other kids as we all tried to grab the ring in the middle. By the time the ride was over I almost forgot about running away.

Alden sat on the park bench watching. It had been so long since I'd seen my big brother smile, I'd forgotten what his teeth looked like. I told him I wasn't mad anymore, which was a good thing because it just then started to rain. I put his red hunting hat on his head and smacked a kiss on his cheek and went for another ride on the carousel, picking a white horse this time. No matter how much I urged him, Alden didn't want to ride. He was content to watch.

He just sat in the rain, watching me ride. And—I learned yesterday—he found happiness in that moment.

When I finished reading that chapter, I cried and cried. I couldn't bring myself to read any more, even though there was only one chapter left.

Oh, Alden! I wish I could hug that sixteen-year-old boy and tell him it will be okay. But, of course, I cannot promise him, or you, anything. Here you are—a forty-year-old man—and I still want to take care of you. But I can't, can I? You are an adult. You are your own person. I cannot pave your life's path with bricks of gold. And I cannot be sure anything will be okay in your world. No matter what I do.

The ice cream has melted on the table in front of me. I shove the entire sloshy box into the freezer and make my way upstairs, feeling that with each step I get closer to making peace with my childhood and embracing who I am today. Wife, sister, daughter. Someday, maybe a mother.

I find myself in my bathroom, blinking against the light, suddenly too bright. The test results are there on the counter.

I have to pluck the box out of the trash to read the instructions; it occurs to me I don't even remember what a positive result is supposed to look like. I read the blurb on the box and compare the picture diagram with my own test.

They match.

Chapter 21
Jerry

Even when the plane is at full altitude, I still can't believe it. Alden and his biracial girlfriend are four rows behind me. Alden's waving money at the stewardess like he's at a ball game.

"Another round of Bloodies, please!"

This is going to be the longest flight of my life.

Alden hasn't spoken to me since our argument the night he read the galley. He stormed off, slamming the spare-room door with such gusto the whole apartment shook. I wallowed where I was in that dreadful butterfly chair all night long. That was two months ago. To say it's been tense in the apartment, living with someone who won't speak to you, is a huge understatement.

The book launched last month. It's out in print. Out in the world. I'm en route to my book tour Fiona has set up for me. At her insistence, Alden is here too. This is going to be so awkward.

"Business or pleasure?" says the guy next to me, an older gentleman who holds a bowler hat on his lap. He just finished a very ripe banana and now the whole plane smells of it.

"Huh? Oh. Business, I guess."

He gives a throaty chortle. "Back in my day, we wore suits when we traveled for business. I'll never get used to this. Although I never imagined they'd have microwave ovens that can cook an egg in less than a minute. Amazing."

I ignore him. I really don't want to talk about modern technology. I don't even care if I'm rude.

Kiki's giggles make their way to our row. Surely, Alden told her some juvenile joke. I can tell by the way he keeps saying, "What's so funny?" in that mock-serious tone. I feel like I'm in a side show at the damn circus.

"Ah, kids," my neighbor says.

I want to correct him: *No, sir. That's my brother who's nearly forty.* But I don't. Because it's true. Alden is just a kid.

"You have any children?" he says.

I shake my head in what I hope is a conversation-ending way and open my *Newsweek*, even though the words are all black ants to me. All done with small talk, banana guy.

How did I get so miserable? I'm not sure I can count a single happy moment since Janine.

Janine.

I close my eyes and think of her. I wonder if seeing my little sister, knowing she's pregnant, will make me regret. I don't know.

It wasn't that I didn't want a baby. I did. But I didn't *need* a baby to be happy, like she seemed to. I mean, I would've been content to live out our lives as a twosome—traveling the world, having spontaneous date nights without having to line up a sitter, making love in the middle of the day, decorating the house with as many breakable items as we liked. But Janine wasn't content. Not even close. She became obsessed. Having a baby was all she thought about. It took precedence over every other important thing in our lives. Like the *M*A*S*H* fiasco.

My stress level erupted as my career tanked—no contracts, no work for months. My name seemed to be blacklisted from nearly every studio. It was bad. And our finances? The well had all but dried up. Grandma Gallagher's inheritance was wasted on an apartment complex in the Bronx, which was burned to the ground before I got it insured. Not only was my bank account in the red, proving what a failure I was as a writer, but I also saw it every day in Janine's face, how much I failed her, was failing her every day.

"I need you, Jerry," she'd say all the time, especially after another miscarriage. "You'll get another job," she'd tell me, dismissing it like it wasn't the colossal problem it was.

"We might not be able to have a *family*, Jerry. Why don't you focus on that?"

It was true. Something about us wasn't working. We got pregnant okay. It was staying pregnant that was the problem. Our doctor couldn't identify the problem, which only made Janine's anxiety fester and her impatience with me explode. It didn't matter. We kept losing our babies.

How many times did she miscarry? Each time was different. It all sucked. It did. It was raw. Each was a death we had to grieve alone. Just because Janine didn't see my tears doesn't mean I never cried. Especially after our daughter, our Jade. Sweet baby Jade. I could weep just thinking about her. All two precious pounds of her. Our angel. It just seemed unconscionable that Janine wanted to try again after that. I couldn't put my wife through any more pain like that.

I had to hold it together. Someone had to hold it together. We were falling apart. I was trying to be strong. I thought it was the right thing to do. I thought that's what we needed. What Janine needed.

After Jade, though, Janine decided I was the last thing she needed.

My turn to wave money at the stewardess.

"Budweiser, please."

Maybe that will cheer me up. I'll make it through Alden's wrath. I'll make it through the book tour. And then I'm hanging it up. I'll get a regular office job someplace. Write copy for an ad firm. Or, heck, maybe drive a delivery truck. God knows I can't write anymore. You can't write when there's nothing in your soul.

We land smoothly, taxi the runway. We walk off the jetway into the gate at Logan Airport and Fiona is there with David. They already look like a family. I search myself for jealousy and it's not there. I actually feel good. I open my arms as I approach her, but her hug is brief and she's got this eager look on her face, like we're late for something.

"Hurry!" she says. "I have an interview set up for Alden that starts in thirty minutes."

For *Alden*?

Chapter 22
Fiona

"We can't be late for this interview," I say again. "Did you check bags?"

On my signal, David runs to get the car and our guests—Jerry, Alden, and that pretty Latino girl (whoever she is)—just stare at me. Am I speaking in tongues?

"*Alden* has an interview, you said?" Jerry says, his entire face a squint.

I ignore him. "Okay, David's pulling the car around. He should be at the curb by the time we collect the luggage." I talk over my shoulder as I lead us to baggage claim. Thankfully, everyone follows. "Your flight was forty-five minutes late. Shoot." I hold the face of my watch as if I could slow it down.

"Fiona, wait," Jerry calls.

"We'll talk in the car," I call to him over my shoulder.

At baggage claim, waiting for the luggage to appear, Alden appears at my side. I lean against him and start to relax, or try to. Stress is no good for the baby; I know that much. But if they only *knew* how hard I worked to get this interview!

Alden squeezes my shoulders.

"How ya feelin', sis? How's the little kicker?"

There's no use fighting my smile as I instinctively put a hand on my belly. "I can't wait to feel kicks."

His boyish grin is all love. "Is it a boy or girl? What do you think?"

"I'm not going to say. It might be bad luck."

"I think it's a boy."

"I think it's a girl."

"Thought you weren't gonna say?"

"Whoops." I let myself smile, hugging that familiar, lanky body of my brother's again. His usual smell of old laundry and cigarettes is mixed with reprocessed air and tomato juice. Resting my head on his shoulder, I've all but forgotten the others when Alden's girlfriend leans in. "Hi, I'm Kiki."

"Fiona." We shake. "Nice to meet you in person. I didn't realize Alden was bringing anyone."

"Oh, Alden insisted. I have a sister in New York that I haven't seen in ages. He's arranged a reunion, I guess." She covers a shy smile with her hand. "I promise I won't be any trouble."

"Welcome," I say. If Alden brought her she must be important to him, but it makes me wonder: Does Alden know this is a business trip? He really shouldn't have any distractions. He will be an active participant in this tour.

"I think that's everything," Jerry says, surrounded by suitcases.

"Great. Let's go!" To my relief, everyone comes to attention, handles in hand. Well, almost everyone.

"Wait. I can't find mine." Kiki scans the luggage on the carousel while I check my watch. We don't have time for this. I'm growling inside; I can't blame pregnancy for this kind of cranky.

"What color is it?" Jerry asks.

"Black."

"Oh dear," I say. A river of black suitcases glides by. This could take hours. I tug Alden's shirt and whisper, "Listen, David is waiting. Why don't we let them figure this luggage thing out and we'll come back for them? Or send a cab. We really need to get to this interview."

Alden gives me an easy smile as if he doesn't have a care in the world. And he doesn't. He practically shouts: "Aw, we can't leave without Kiki."

Jerry and Kiki turn toward us, disbelief frozen on their faces. Something like a laugh erupts from my embarrassment, and I pull on Alden's shirt again, harder this time. "Can we—"

"There it is!" Kiki exclaims.

We squeeze the luggage, and ourselves, into David's car. I wish I had known there would be an extra person. Sensing my tension, David takes my hand. Three squeezes. I reciprocate at record squeeze speed. As he pulls away, I spin to face the crew in the back.

"Wait!" Alden is about to light up a cigarette. "Please, not in the car. And not around the baby, if you don't mind." It dawns on me that besides my husband, I may be the only responsible person here.

Alden apologizes and puts it away. He doesn't seem to mind.

"Okay," I say. "Let's talk about our plan here. It was a bit of a challenge, but I've booked some key interviews to kick off our tour. So thank you in advance for helping us be punctual to all our appointments. I know you all understand how important this is. Alden, in about twenty minutes you have an interview with the *Boston Herald*.

We're on our way to Dunkin Donuts, where we'll meet Karen Carter who will write a feature article on you and your story. It will be in Sunday's paper—which is great—in the Arts section."

Alden holds up a hand, looking confused—and then it's like a bolt of joy hits him. "Oh, is this for my book, *Allie*?"

He can't be serious. "No, this is for...Jerry's book."

Why did I say that? It's not Jerry's book!

"Then why am I being interviewed?"

I study my brother to gauge whether or not he's playing with me, as he's wont to do. I squirm self-consciously and glance at Kiki. I'm assuming Alden has told her, if she's come all this way. Still, I opt for civility.

"Because, Alden," I say with forced composure, "it is customary to interview the author."

Alden reaches into his knapsack and retrieves one of the galleys. His voice is all sarcasm. "Jerry's named *himself* as the author, Fiona. It's right here. In print. Bam!"

He's all hard angles; his anger is obviously raw. Jerry, on the other side of Kiki, is looking out the window. Oh, no. Jerry didn't tell him the whole truth. Couldn't have. This tour is going to be a challenge.

"Alden, I know we didn't get a chance to talk about the plan, but...I mean, we all know now that *you* are the one who should be interviewed. Period."

"Don't you think that's going to be...confusing?" Alden gives me an exaggerated grin and I realize this is all for Jerry's benefit. Wonderful! In addition to managing this tour and my morning sickness, I'm going to have to decipher Alden's passive-aggressive digs on Jerry.

Alden turns his clown-smile to Jerry, whose face is impassive but beet-red. "Don't you think that will be *confusing*, Jerry?"

"Yeah." Jerry's voice is barely audible.

"Word. So how does that work, Jerry? It's totally a problem, right?"

This car is too small for this. Even if Jerry made an enormous mistake, he is still my oldest brother and I can't stand seeing him attacked like this.

"Hold on," I say, looking pointedly at Alden. "Here is the plan, okay? You *both* will sit for the interviews. You will act as though it's been…a collaboration from day one." I hold my breath waiting for them to react.

"We're co-authors, then?" Jerry asks.

"That's not going to work," Alden says. "It's not my name—"

"A glitch in printing," I say with a wave of my hand. "Something we can address."

Everyone's quiet for a while. As the car turns off the exit ramp, I'm pulled toward David who supports me with his upper arm. Kiki sees this and gives me an approving smile. Maybe it is a good thing she's here.

"Or…" Alden says thoughtfully. "Or I don't have to be named an *author* specifically."

I frown at him. Please, Alden, take a stand for your intellectual property!

"We could say Jerry was my, like, ghostwriter, right? Like, I hired him to write my story. Isn't that what a ghostwriter does?"

Jerry shakes his head. "If I were the ghostwriter, Alden's name would still be listed as the author even if I wrote it."

Alden's expression hardens. I interrupt before he can respond.

"I know what you mean, though. Semantics aside, let that be our story. Alden hired his brother, his Hollywood writer brother, to author his story. His memoir."

Alden clamps his jaw. "Still. It's not like I would *need* his help."

Jerry glumly stares out the window. "Usually celebrities or politicians hire ghost writers—"

I sigh. "Guys, please! We all know the truth here. I'm not suggesting this is what actually happened. We just need a story. We need to protect ourselves. The media gets ahold of the truth and it won't look good for *anyone*."

"We're almost there," David interjects.

"Can we agree on our story, please?" I beg my beloved, frustrating-as-anything brothers.

By a miracle, we arrive at Dunkin Donuts before Karen Carter. The guys buy coffee while Kiki and I head for the ladies' room. I feel like I've been holding it for a week. I'm not in the mood for "urination conversation" as Linda would call it, but Kiki apparently is. She talks right over the sound of our streams, but I don't respond.

"Do you think you might have some contacts?" she asks my reflection as we wash our hands.

"Excuse me?"

"For *Allie*. He was hoping you would have some publishing contacts. Even if it's a small company. Alden just wants to see it in print."

Huh. This young lady does care about my brother. I feel a surge of warmth toward her. "Kiki, how long have you and Alden been dating?"

"Oh, we're just good friends. We tried the dating thing, but we didn't fit very well."

Why would Alden bring a girl here if she wasn't *his* girl? And what an odd thing to say, they "didn't fit very well." Oh. I blush and try to erase the picture that's popped into my mind. "I'd love to help Alden too," I say quickly. "Let's get this tour underway and then we can talk about *Allie*. I can only focus on one book at a time." I'm touching my stomach, and I hear myself murmur, "Though lately, it seems difficult to focus on anything, really."

Kiki tells me she understands, smiling shyly.

Karen Carter is greeting the guys when we emerge from the restroom. I hurry to Alden's side, taking his arm to emphasize *he* is the important one. I'm willing eye contact with Karen, but her eyes are locked on Jerry.

"So Jerry," Karen says. "Let's get this interview started. I prefer one-on-one. Let's sit at a table in the back, if you don't mind."

I step forward and shake Karen's hand, reminding her of who I am. "Karen, this is my other brother, Alden Gallagher. He is the subject of the book. It is his story. Jerry just…authored it."

Karen looks at Alden, then back at Jerry. To me, she says, "I understood there was one author."

"Two for the price of one!" Alden announces, beaming at her.

Karen gives a Mona Lisa and sighs. "Well, then. Let's get on with it."

I watch the three of them head to the back of the shop. Karen marches officiously, Alden saunters as if he's window shopping on a Sunday afternoon, and Jerry slumps like a reluctant captive. God, this has to work.

Then Jerry turns and waves at me before taking his seat next to Alden. Why did he do that? I can see him in profile, a weary observer. As I sink down at my own table, I'm reminded that my oldest brother is close to fifty. Tenderness lifts my heart. Ever since I was little, I always pictured Jerry as an able-bodied soldier, healthy and strong. But here he is: His entire expression, his entire aura, droops with exhaustion. I think of our latest talk, the fight we had over the phone. Poor thing, he's been holding onto so much anger. For years. My heart hurts thinking about it.

Alden and Karen settle into a comfortable question-and-answer volley, and Jerry glances back again—ever the watchful big brother.

This time I smile broadly, give him a thumbs-up.

Chapter 23
Alden

That was not fun.

Geez, it's been so long I thought it wouldn't bother me, but once that Karen Carter started in with the questions it all came back as if it were real-time. Just rolled in like dirty fog over the ocean. Through the whole interview, I wanted to throw my fist into Jerry's ear. That shit I pulled at sixteen is humiliating. What a sad, lying sack I was. A total downer to even think about.

And—*bam!*—now Fiona tells me I gotta read it *aloud* to an audience? No way, José. I'm handing it over. Jerry, go nuts. You wanted it so bad, take it. It's yours.

Fiona fought me on the train in to Boston, but she's got to have a clue that this shit is embarrassing. She finally relented, but begged me to choose the part Jerry reads. Nope. Not doing that either.

But then, what part does Jerry choose? The part with the prostitute. I mean, after the prostitute when that goddam elevator guy socked me a bruiser. As if the prostitute part wasn't lame enough, the whole world will know I got socked by her pimp. If that doesn't sting enough—I didn't even get laid out of the deal—Fiona supports Jerry's choice. Claims it shows vulnerability, which will get people to "empathize." Totally bogus. All I know is, Fiona forgets what a doggish, pansy-ass fool our brother is. It's like she's trying to make up for how much I hate the bastard, like those two are in cahoots.

Makes me kinda ticked at Fiona, my favorite person, which is depressing as hell.

So I'm not even going to be in the goddam room while Jerry reads the thing. I flat-out refuse.

I'm outside Bachman Bookshop now. Slipped out before Jerry started. I motioned for Kiki to come with, but she wanted to hear the excerpt. Don't blame her, really. I mean, she can read the whole goddam thing if she wants to. No one's stopping her. I'm just not going to sit there *waiting* for her reaction while she does it. You couldn't pay me to do that.

So I'm outside having a smoke when this dude comes up to me. I'd say he's, like, mid-thirties, kind of on the heavy side, with mousy-brown hair and big brown-rimmed glasses. He's wearing a black trench coat and this fur hat like they wear in Russia.

"Did it start yet? Did I miss it?" he asks me, clutching a book—*Jerry's* book—in his hands.

"Miss what? The reading?"

He nods like mad. Even though it's cold, guy's sweating. His glasses slide down his nose and he shoves them back. Maybe give the furry hat a break, I would say. But it suits his babyish moon-face.

"No," I say. "I mean, it did start. But it *just* started."

Here's the funny thing: He touches me on the shoulder, like I just saved his goddam life, and thanks me up and down. I kinda laugh, and he laughs too. It's the kind of moment that used to link us hippies back in the day— stronger than clothes or drugs or anything else. It was that kind of synchronized laugh.

He tips his furry Russian hat and says in a really bad British accent, "Thank ye! G'daye sir!"

What a goofball! At the same time, I'm grateful, since he totally cheered me up. Dude boogies inside. He has the book in his hand, waving it around like a cautionary flag. Cracks me up. The book just came out and he's, like, all over it. It's a miracle anyone's even read the thing, much less *liked* it.

I kick pebbles around on the concrete while I finish my smoke. Through the glass, I see Jerry's still reading. The furry-hat dude is toward the back, a daffed-out look on his face, as if he's listening to the word of God. He's holding the book in prayer hands. That kills me.

I figure what I'll do is walk around Downtown Crossing and see if there's a pharmacy or convenience store. I forgot to pack a toothbrush. I can't stand it when that happens. You go on this trip across country and you think about everything: how many socks and underwear you'll need, all that jazz. I even brought my *Allie* manuscript even though Fiona has one. So you get everything into this suitcase, and you forget your toothbrush. Go figure.

I find one pretty close, which is groovy because the place is a mob scene. I'm not keen on big crowds. It's funny because you'd think, growing up in New York City, I'd revel in the pulse of a hopping city. I do just fine, don't get me wrong. I just prefer a more chill mode. I mean, for real, what's the rush?

I buy two pink toothbrushes, in case Kiki wants one. I'm still so glad she's here. No way would I have gone on this trip without her. "I need a sidekick," I told her. She laughed and gave me every excuse on the planet. It wasn't until I thought of a reunion with Kristin that she finally agreed. Don't tell her this—but I kinda fibbed about already having something set up with her sister. Kiki got so excited; she went spazzy. Word. I totally plan on calling Kristin to get the meeting all set. But I'm a little yellow about it now. I mean, I have no idea what kind of chick Kiki's sister is. It was selfish of me, I know. But I think she's having a stellar time with all of us anyway.

There's another reason I need a sidekick. I don't even want to mention my worst fear: running into Teresa. If that happens, I will hide behind Kiki's sweet, wide ass. No kidding. And here's a bonus: Kiki laughs at all my jokes. Even the not-funny ones. It's good for my ego.

I'm on my way back from the pharmacy, weaving through throngs of shoppers, when some dude thumps his hand on my chest. Stops me dead in my tracks. I look up, kinda ticked. It's the furry-hat dude! My laugh is automatic—offering that thing that connected us.

"You!" he says, like he just won the lottery. "You're the brother!"

That stops me cold. "What?"

"The author said, during the reading, he owed it all to his brother, who was out having a smoke." He points with his hand, which is wrapped in a wrist brace. He's got a Southern drawl, which I hadn't noticed before. And his smile—although as broad as the Sargasso Sea—ends with his mouth, like his eyes aren't invited to the party.

He goes on: "He said it was *your* story he documented for you. It says in the acknowledgments that you were the inspiration for it all. But it's more than that. It's you! It's you, isn't it? It's got to be. Wow. I can't believe it. I met you before I even met him."

I cringe inside, wishing a wall of steel between me and that goddam book. I feel my face fall, so I turn away. But he keeps right up with me. I mean, he seems cool. You'd think he would run the other way knowing I was the true narrator of that book. But it's like it's a *good* thing, in his mind. Never thought that would happen.

"And I thought I was late!" he says. "Thank goodness I was late. I may never have met you!"

"Yo, we actually haven't met," I say, pausing on the sidewalk to extend my hand.

Furry-hat dude slaps his own forehead. "I'm so sorry!" But he doesn't look sorry. "I'm MD." He takes my hand, the Velcro on his wrist-brace scratching my fingertips.

"MD?" I ask.

"No, I'm not a doctor." He laughs, sounding like a little girl this time, making me giggle too. As if we're both high as a kite.

"I didn't think you were a doctor," I say, still laughing.

"I'm an acronym! Just like your brother. He uses his initials for the book, so I'm using mine. But my wife calls me Mark."

"Hi, Acronym. Or should I call you Mark?"

We both have a giggle fit again.

"Call me MD. But what's your name? Do you go by Holden?"

My laughter drops fast as a hiccup. "No, no. It's Alden."

"Of course," he says, eyeing me in a way that makes me self-conscious. I kinda finger-comb my hair and head to Bachman Bookshop.

"So, are you going along for the whole tour?" he asks, staying with me.

I don't answer. MD's voice softens. "I want you to know that you have a supporter here. I've come a long way. I live in Honolulu. I—"

"Hawaii?" I say. "I've never been, but—that accent? I would've put money on you being from the South."

"Oh, that. Yeah, I'm originally from Georgia…" His words drop off and it's like a hood comes down over his eyes.

I bring him back to sunshine. "So, Honolulu, huh? You didn't come all this way to get your book signed, did you?" I kinda laugh when I say this; it sounds so zappy.

"Yes!" He brightens again. "Actually, I have two reasons for coming to the mainland. One: to get my book signed. Two: I want to meet John Lennon."

Now I really crack up. "Really? But Lennon isn't in Boston—"

"I'm taking a train to New York. I know where he lives. I've been reading about his life in the penthouse of the Dakota building near Central Park." He sighs to the sky.

"We're headed to New York, too. You know, for the tour."

"Oh!" he exclaims. He eyes me and whispers, "Synchronicity."

Not sure why all the heavy, but I lighten the mood. "A book signed by my brother and an autograph by Lennon? Pretty odd pairing."

"Oh, no." His face is serious. "No, it makes perfect sense. The two are linked—"

"Alden?" It's Fiona, interrupting us just when it gets interesting. I focus on MD, though, waiting for him to finish. No luck. He's buttoned up his lips and his eyes are on Fiona, grinning like a cat and blinking super-fast, like he's trying to dislodge a speck of sand.

"I didn't know where you went," she says, ignoring my new friend. "Jerry's finished and has already gone to the next interview. I thought we could meet him there and grab a quick bite before heading home."

I'm about to introduce her to MD when he jumps in. "Oh, would you mind terribly if I tag along?" he says. "It's just that I've traveled so far and…oh, it would mean the world to me. The world! This book has changed my life already."

They swap hellos. Fiona's eyes get big when she realizes he came all the way from Hawaii for *this book*. She invites him to join us, smiling and taking his arm. I lag behind. I'd rather eat dirt than do another interview with Jerry about the goddam book. But now I feel kinda responsible for this furry-hat dude, coming all the way from Hawaii for this book. And to meet John Lennon! It's like he's a big kid who still believes in Santa Claus. Makes you want to go along with it just so he'll keep believing. I get a little pang for Daniel. Hope the little dude is doing okay. So, now I'm all mushy inside and going along to the next interview.

Kiki's here now and she's got this look on her face I don't copy. She hugs my hips as we follow behind Fiona and MD. Kiki whispers, "I'm so proud of you, I can't even stand it."

"Yeah?" I grin at the pavement. Even though I don't want anything to do with the book, this totally makes me feel good. I hold onto that feeling as we walk along Boston Common, making our way to the Park Plaza.

I'm just grateful Jerry has gone ahead without me. Hopefully, he's done with the interview by the time I get there.

Chapter 24
Jerry

Just when I think I've got a handle on our shtick, someone throws me a curveball. This Brad Heffernan from the *Globe* is nothing like Karen Carter from the *Herald*. With Karen it felt like we were helping her out with a book report. This guy is asking some odd questions, like he's got a mystery to figure out.

We sit in the main lounge of the Boston Park Plaza Hotel. The piano in the corner makes me think of an upscale Ernie's in New York, but no one's playing at the moment. The place is like my parents' country club we used to go to for brunch when we were younger. I tend to avoid fancy places like this. Since my time in the military, it just doesn't feel right—all this extravagance.

With an interview and reading under my belt, I'm comfortable enough to order a vodka tonic. That was a mistake. Brad has a Tab in front of him, and he hasn't even touched it. He's wearing a suit, and doesn't take off his jacket. He doesn't look at me when he shakes my hand, nor does he when asking his questions. Even though I'm the one being interviewed, he looks uncomfortable.

I apologize for my brother's truancy, and Brad blinks at me coolly. He doesn't seem like the kind of guy who likes to wait around for anyone.

"So, Mr. Gallagher, you've built your career as a screenwriter. Why the shift to fiction?"

My conversation with Mitch comes to mind, when I told him I wanted to convert it to a screenplay. "Fuck no," was his response. If I share this with Brad Heffernan, he might ask more questions about Hollywood. Next thing you know, I'll be reliving the whole *M*A*S*H* fiasco in the *Boston Globe*.

"Please call me Jerry. Well, writing for movies and television is fast-paced and exciting. But this is something that's been years in the making. It's nice to have something done on my own timeline. Something personal." I'm surprised he accepts this vague and slightly dishonest answer so readily.

He's still writing in his notebook when he asks: "Tell me, what kind of social criticism are you trying to achieve here?"

"Social criticism?" I stifle a laugh. "This could hardly be considered—"

"But you continually use a specific term: *phony*. You basically accuse others of being insincere and disingenuous repeatedly throughout the novel."

"Well, my main character does."

Brad looks dubious, but lets it go. "Yes. Let's talk about him. Your main character is a loner, to be blunt. Would you say he alienates himself from others or do others alienate him?"

"Um, I guess a little of both."

"You guess?"

"I mean, he alienates himself."

"Right. From the same society in which he criticizes."

"Sure. Okay."

"How would you describe your main character?" Brad cocks his head at me.

"How do you mean?"

"As a person. Some would suggest he is condescending, arrogant. How would you describe him?"

"He's just a kid." Now I'm feeling defensive. This is *Alden* we're talking about. "I would describe him as troubled."

"But, at sixteen, he would be old enough to recognize that his blanket judgments on the rest of the society are, should we say, narrow-minded."

"I don't know of any sixteen-year-old kid who has that kind of self-awareness. But I guess someone could see it that way."

"Is there another way to see it?" He doesn't wait for my answer. "Do you worry about backlash?"

"Backlash?"

Brad blinks fast. "Some may petition to have it banned."

Now I do laugh. "Banned? You're kidding!"

"Some people—especially parents—may be offended with your main character's questionable morals and behavior."

"Actually, I don't believe his behavior is necessarily immoral."

"Really? He lies, smokes. He's inappropriate toward girls." Brad straightens his jacket.

"If you look beyond what he says, and look at what he does, you see he's not a bad kid."

"But you can't deny the language could be considered offensive. And the casual discussion of teenage sex. Some people may think you're condoning it."

"Well, as I said, actions speak louder than words. My main character is a virgin. And despite being…impatient with some, he's typically respectful toward girls and women."

Brad takes a moment to scratch something in his notebook. He's got this terrific frown on his face. Man, he's all bent out of shape about this book. I had no idea it could garner such a reaction. He seems personally insulted. And he's a journalist? So much for being objective, I guess. I take a minute to size him up. He's well groomed and athletic-looking. Thick neck and all. He wears a wedding ring and I wonder if he has children. Maybe that's it. He's nervous about his own son growing up and making mistakes like Alden did. Doesn't he know everyone makes mistakes? I'll bet he did. Maybe he went wild in his college fraternity. Maybe he ruined an athletic scholarship in the process. Baseball, probably. That's why he's so worried. He doesn't want his kid to do what he did. Probably has nothing to do with Alden *or* the book.

Brad's next question takes on a scholarly tone. "There seems to be a very 'us versus them' tone in the novel. Meaning 'kid versus adult.'"

I hadn't thought about it before, but now that he says it, I realize it's true, and say as much. "According to my main character, adults and kids exist in separate worlds. But that's not to imply kids are good and adults are evil.

Just…different. Like, they have different frameworks for reality."

He looks at me evenly, his pen poised at his notebook. "How do you hope to help young people with this novel?"

This sort of throws me off. He just warned me that the book may be banned, and now he asks how it might help kids. I fill the silence with a long drink of my vodka tonic, and my mind turns to Allie and his alphabet, Alden in that psych ward, Fiona's baby…

"I hope to encourage kids to be proud of themselves," I say. "I want to give hope to those not in the in-crowd that life doesn't begin and end at school. I want to reach all the kids who may not be into academics or athletics, per se, but have other non-traditional talents. Encourage them. I hope kids embrace their childhood, cherish it. Don't rush to grow up, like so many of us do."

He scoffs. It's just a hint, but I see it. "You really think kids will take all that away from this book?"

I shrug. "My main character, he's not a bad kid."

"You said your brother was your inspiration for that character."

"Yep. It's actually his story. I wrote it for him," I say, a swell of affection welling my chest. "He's a great guy."

As if on cue, Alden comes in. Kiki's there too, followed by Fiona and this guy wearing a Russian fur hat I recognize from the reading earlier. What an odd collection of people. I wave them over and say to Brad, "Here he is now. You can ask him anything. He lived it."

Fiona shakes Brad's hand and apologizes for interrupting. *No worries, Fiona*, I think. Brad may not be

165

done torturing me, but I am through with him. I convince the entire group to join us in hopes Brad will get the hint and shove off. I do introductions, but when I get to the heavy-set guy with the glasses and the fur hat, I have to wait for an explanation.

"Oh, this is MD," Fiona says. "He is our number-one fan!"

The guy, MD, jumps in then. "Yes, yes! I am so excited! I met you only briefly at the signing. But now we can sit and talk. And I got to meet your brother, the inspiration—"

Alden waves as if he's on a parade float, but it's obvious he doesn't want to be here. Brad is watching him intensely. I see my brother the way he must: disheveled, with an attitude. I feel obligated to say something in his defense. "We just flew in this morning from California," I say. "No one's really dressed for the Park Plaza."

"Nonsense," Fiona says. "There is no dress code here. We are fine. Who wants something to eat? I was thinking of getting some appetizers to share."

Brad declines, claiming he can't stay. MD, removing his fur hat with a flourish, insists on buying us all a round of drinks. He then orders three shrimp cocktails and Heinekens for everyone.

Brad puts his notebook back in his briefcase. He shakes my hand again and thanks me. I'm relieved to see him go, but then Fiona says, "Brad, did you know MD came all the way from Honolulu to meet Jerry and Alden?"

"You're kidding."

MD raises his right hand. "So help me God."

To my dismay, Brad takes out his notebook again and turns to MD. "No offense to the author, but why such an extravagant effort to meet him?"

MD pushes his glasses back. "I haven't been able to stop reading the book since I got it. I talk about it to whoever will listen. It's an extraordinary book that holds many answers."

Brad scribbles on his notebook. Alden smiles at this stranger from Honolulu, who seems to have completely won him over. Our order comes and there is a polite silence as the waitress settles parfaits of jumbo shrimp and five beers on our small cocktail table.

"Not to diminish the piece," says Brad. "But what is prompting such a passionate reaction?"

"Just brilliant social commentary," he says in a calm Southern drawl. "This is the first book I've read that has had such an effect on me—I feel like it speaks to me directly." He chuckles. "Oh, gosh, now I sound crazy. What I mean is, I really connect with Holden. I feel like he and I are...kindred spirits."

Fiona's eyes go wide. Kiki gives a nervous giggle.

MD fans the pages of his book, which are underlined, highlighted, and annotated. "Like when he talks about the Museum of Natural History..." He flips to one of his marked pages and starts reading aloud:

"*The best thing, though, in that museum was that everything always stayed right where it was. Nobody'd move. You could go there a hundred thousand times, and that Eskimo would still be just finished catching those two fish, the birds would still be on their way south, the deers would still be drinking out of that water hole, with their pretty antlers and their pretty, skinny legs, and that squaw with the naked bosom would still be weaving that same blanket. Nobody'd be different. The only thing that would be different would be* you.'"

He slowly closes the book and caresses the cover. "Brilliant."

Fiona keeps checking on Alden, who astonishingly seems to be enjoying the recitation of his teenage journal. Perhaps because I'm not the one reading it?

"MD, I find this extremely interesting," Brad says. "Could you tell me, please, how does it speak to you personally? In what way do you connect with its message?"

"Oh my Holy Lord!" MD exclaims. "It's so raw and beautiful. This kid is drowning in the challenges of an adult world, a world that cannot be trusted. Where everything changes on a dime. The one you love doesn't love you back. People get sick, move away, loved ones die. This kid is in search for answers, but all he wants is peace. All he wants is to protect what's innocent in the world, because eventually everything that's innocent gets tainted, or destroyed. See, in this museum, he loves that everything is still and calm and unchanging. Kind of like that poem by Keats, *Ode on a Grecian Urn*. Do you know it? He describes all these images on this urn, and envies them because they'll always be just as they are. And will never change. *When old age shall this generation waste, Thou shalt remain, in midst of other woe...*"

Fiona looks as if she's swallowed a shrimp's tail. She coughs until her eyes are wet. Brad has stopped writing.

He clears his throat and says with suppressed incredulity, "Are you making a literary comparison between this book and John Keats's *Ode on a Grecian Urn*?"

MD laughs and I'm shocked (but also relieved) to see Alden laughing too. "Not the whole book. Just that passage about the museum."

Brad rearranges his tie. "I was going to say...that would be something. To make such a comparison would be—"

"I know," MD says. "It doesn't do it justice. This book is far more important than some silly poem written in the eighteen hundreds."

At that, Brad is speechless. For the first time since we started this tour, I feel myself smile.

Chapter 25
Fiona

I'm astonished—and absolutely pleased—at our new acquaintance's enthusiasm for the book. It's like a child about Disneyland, even more so. The *Globe* reporter appeared to dismiss MD's praise of it, although he did capture what was said into his notebook. I'd been unsure, but now I'm looking forward to reading his story. I'm hoping for a placement in the Sunday Arts section.

After an awkward goodbye, Brad has taken his briefcase and gone. Alden high-fives MD, and Jerry is grinning for the first time since the plane landed. The five of us linger at the Park Plaza a bit longer—though the shrimp cocktail is long gone. A comfortable quiet settles around us as the boys and Kiki sip their Heinekens. Our number-one fan, it seems, has turned our family starry-eyed. I can almost feel the animosity dissipating as the three of us see the book through his eyes.

"David should be here soon," I say. "Is there somewhere we can drop you, MD? I hate to leave you like this."

"Oh, don't you worry about me," he says. "I think I'll rough it here at the Park Plaza."

That makes us all laugh. Jerry offers to wait outside to keep an eye out for David: "I've been sitting in this chair long enough. It'll be good to stretch my legs."

After he's gone, Alden tugs Kiki's hand, suggesting a tour of the hotel. MD watches them go, then turns to me eagerly. "Fiona, you mentioned that you were doing the publicity for the book, which has gotten me thinking. It's so very exciting. What are your plans to promote it?"

"I…" He's caught me off-guard. I wonder why he wants to know. "Well, we have the tour," I hedge, maintaining poise. "Which consists of signings and readings…interviews of course. I've written some press releases. That sort of thing. Standard stuff."

MD stares at the chandelier. "I think you need something bigger," he says softly.

"Well, I'm working with some of the big name bookstores, like B. Dalton, to get some good shelf space. But it's tough going because they need to justify that with sales. It's really too early to measure that."

"I think we need to be more creative," he says, hunching toward me. He keeps glancing at the book, which is cradled in his palms, as if to make sure it hasn't disappeared. Why is he talking about "we"?

I try to brush him off. "MD, you've helped quite a bit with Mr. Heffernan here. You've done more than we'd ever ask of a fan."

But he goes on as if I haven't spoken. "What about schools? How about getting it into high school curricula?"

This makes me laugh. "I'm touched by your vote of confidence. We all are, but—"

"It's important!" he presses. "It should be read by every person in this country. The world!"

I offer a polite smile and scan the lobby for Alden and Kiki.

"I'm sorry," MD says, his eyes dipping. "It's just my excitement. I shouldn't come on so strong. My mother always tells me I don't wear well on people. Perhaps I should go…"

"Oh, MD. It's fine. No worries. I'm tickled by your idea. Perhaps down the road that would be an option. Let's just try to get some sales before…" I bite my lip. Did I just say *let's*?

"Yes!" he says, leaping up. He perches on the edge of his seat, shifting closer to me. "Traditional marketing is too slow. And is not reliable. It doesn't always work. We need a story behind this. Drama. Something we can sell with it. Something that people can't ignore. Shock value. We've got to think shock value."

I feel my jaw drop. But he couldn't possibly know about Jerry's betrayal—unless Alden told him? The glimmer in his eye tells me he knows at least something.

"Alden didn't tell you…about how the book came to be, did he?"

It's like MD's ideas are erased and replaced with new thoughts. He tilts his head at me. "Well, it *is* his story."

My face burns. How dare Alden tell him! "MD, listen…Jerry has been in a rough place. He's had some…personal issues that have clouded his judgment. I know it sounds dubious, but he didn't mean for it to happen this way. If he could turn the tables back, he would never have gone behind Alden's back like that. Because you're right, it's Alden's story. Jerry had no right to it…"

But MD's not looking at me in understanding, just confusion. Then realization unfolds behind his big lenses. Oh, no. What have I done?

"Jerry stole it?" MD's staring at the book now, tracing his finger over Jerry's printed name on the cover.

They must have the heat cranked in this hotel. It's a sauna. I'm gulping for air. The baby is a ball of heat, and I'm having some sort of hormonal reaction. Hot flashes or something. Sweat itches my scalp and builds under my arms. How could I have misread what he said? I don't know what to make of this. I silently admonish myself for betraying my brothers, and to this complete stranger. And he *is* a stranger. We don't know him and cannot trust him. Oh my God—what if he leaks this to the press?

I don't know what to do other than to plead with him. "Okay, how about this. Let's forget this whole conversation. Please. I don't need any more trouble with my family. Honestly, MD. You have no idea. I need them to work together on this. Especially if we want to sell this book." I'm scrambling. And so I use what I know MD wants. "MD, you want to see this book sell, and so do I. Please. Don't mention this."

My heart pounds in my chest, which feels as hollow as a drum. I watch him open the book, bring it to his nose and take a whiff.

"We need to get attention to this book—quickly." His voice is urgent. He's perspiring and his breathing is labored, as if he'd just sprinted up a flight of stairs.

I remain completely still. Maybe he'll forget I'm even here.

He fans the pages of the book close to his chin, like he's trying to absorb the ink into his pores. He repeats this gesture over and over as he speaks. "We need to do something that makes people see the world differently, like Holden did for me. What is Holden trying to tell us? What call-to-action can be read between the lines? Something to shock them into another realm of consciousness. Something the media cannot ignore. Something bigger than us."

He's in another world, staring into space again. Now, his lips are moving but nothing's coming out. His eyes narrow as if he's focusing on something across the room. I follow his line of vision and see Alden and Kiki near the piano. Alden must be teasing her about sitting to play Chopsticks, because she's laughing and restraining him playfully. MD watches them, an unreadable expression in his eyes, and rubs the book between his palms.

Jerry is suddenly beside me. I jump when he touches my shoulder. "David's here," he says, and then goes to tell Alden and Kiki.

When I turn back to MD, his eyes are wide and focused on mine, a strange smile playing on his lips. "What about a celebrity?"

It's like I've missed part of the conversation, the part when he mumbled to himself. "You mean, a spokesperson?"

"I came to the mainland for two reasons. One: to get my book signed. Two: to meet John Lennon."

"What?" I'm sure I didn't hear him right. "What about John Lennon?"

Jerry is back at my side. Alden and Kiki are on their way out the door, waving goodbye to our new friend. "Come on, Fiona," Jerry says. "Nice to meet you, MD."

Jerry helps me to my feet, and, like a gentleman, holds out his arm for me to take. "Just a minute, Jerry," I say, my voice shaking. "I'll meet you out there."

A flicker of confusion crosses Jerry's face before he shrugs and goes out. Before I can turn my attention back to MD, he's got my hands in his. I'm startled by the sudden physical contact. My wedding ring scratches against his wrist brace.

"Let me handle it," he whispers close, a look of euphoria in his eyes. "I can do it."

"Do what?" I can barely get the words out.

Rather than answer, MD dips his head to settle his fleshy lips on my fingertips. I gasp instinctively, pulling my hand away. He does another odd thing, then. He starts laughing hysterically, flopping into his seat. He's mumbling something. There are words mixed in with the hysteria, but I can't make them out. My mouth goes dry; he seems to no longer realize nor care that I'm in his presence. I back away, keeping my eyes on the back of his head, which is soon covered with the fur hat he wore into the hotel. He's stroking it as his laughter grows and grows. I turn and rush to the exit, checking back only when I've reached the glass doors. He's still sitting there with his back to me, cracking up at who knows what.

Chapter 26
Alden

Ah, I have Fiona's whole goddam palace to myself. Well, not totally. Big Dave is in the front yard raking wet leaves out of a ditch near the foundation. "Fall cleanup," he calls it. But I think he just wants to be outside. New Englanders can get very moody about weather, I kid you not.

Kiki went along with Jerry and Fiona to "western Mass," my sister called it. They're hitting a few colleges out there in the Amherst area. Book signings mostly, some readings. Kiki got all psyched about seeing some New England countryside. She wanted me to come with—begged me actually—but I'm perfectly content handing it over to Jerry. I only wish I could be there to watch him squirm. That's fun.

That MD dude was interesting. Word. Can't believe he loves the book so much. It almost makes me wish I'd made Jerry hand it over to me. Almost. Not sure if MD felt sorry for me or idolized me. I mean, Holden. Oh, well. Too late now. Wonder if he'll have any luck getting Lennon's autograph. He is one jive turkey, that furry hat dude. Cracks me up.

I really just want to put the whole book tour in a drawer and start chugging eggnog. Even though it's only the first weekend in December, Christmas is all over the goddam place. Which is apropos, considering the book is all about

Christmastime too. Wonder if Jerry or Fiona planned it that way.

While they're gone, what I figure I'll do is make some calls. I'd like to check on Daniel. And I have to get with Kiki's sister and set up a meeting. And there's this small publishing firm in Boston who might be interested in *Allie* if I can snow them well enough.

I call information for Kristin Curran in Manhattan. Luck is with me because the next thing I know, this whiny voice gets on the line that must belong to Kiki's blondie sister. She sounds like she just woke up, even though it's almost noon. I introduce myself and explain I have her sister with me in Boston.

"She lives in Boston? I thought she was doing the Californ-i-yay thing."

"No, no. Word. Let me start at the get-go. Kiki and I are friends. We both live in California—"

"Who? Kiki?"

"Kyra. I meant Kyra." Her own sister doesn't know her nickname? "Anyway, we're here in Boston for a book tour."

"Book tour? Whattayatalkin about? I live in New York." Then she repeats herself, stretching it out as if I've never heard of the place: *Neeew Yooorrk*.

"Yeah, I know." Geez, this is harder than I thought. "We're just in Boston for a few days. We go to New York on Monday."

"Like, this Monday? December 5? For real? You're tellin' me my sister is, like, gonna be in New York in two days?"

"That's totally what I'm saying."

A few beats of silence. Then she says, "Are you Kyra's boyfriend or somethin'?"

"No, we're just pals."

But even as I say it I'm grinning like the cat that ate the canary. Kiki and I spooned last night in Fiona's guest bed, and it was delectable. It was a little oven under our covers, and so soft. Her hair smelled like amaretto, brushing against my face, and her generous backside snuggled my balls. Word, don't get me wrong. It wasn't a sexy feeling. But it was probably the most comfortable I've been with a woman, ever. It's scary, though. If she and I ever had a real romantic relationship and it went kaput, we'd no longer be pals. I don't know why relationships have to suck. It almost makes me want to get married. So I wouldn't lose anybody. But look at Janine and Jerry. I guess even marriage isn't a sure thing. Then again, check out Fiona and big Dave. That's one solid couple. They make you want to marry the town spinster.

Kristin's smoking on the other end, making me crave it. Fiona made me promise I wouldn't smoke in the house, so now all I want is to get off the goddam phone with Miss Brains. Time to get a commitment from her. We arrange to meet Tuesday at 10 a.m. at this place called Anton's Diner near her apartment in the Upper East Side.

I go out on the porch to have a smoke.

Big Dave waves to me and marches to the backyard, rake in hand. He's got this spring in his step, like it is spring instead of depressing winter. But it's totally cold. Should've grabbed my jacket. I shiver and get the thing smoked, stamp it out, and put the butt in my pocket.

178

Gotta be careful; these antiques burn like kindling. I'm about to go back into the house when I hear a car pull in. Dude. There's no way they could be back from Amherst already. Maybe they forgot something? What time is it anyway? I forgot to put my watch on this morning. I figure I'll wave hello. I mean, if I had to come all the way back I'd want someone to be there saying hello. But then, it's not them.

"Alden? Is that you?"

Holy shit. What is this? Teresa climbs out of her car and comes up the steps. I am frozen stiff like a corpse.

"Hi there!" she says, all friendly. At least she's dressed properly for winter weather. Big wool coat and scarf and hat and gloves. I just stare at her, shocked as hell, shivering. I think I mutter a hello. Not sure. She's the one with the decent sense to shuffle us inside.

I'm still frozen, though, gaping while she shrugs off her coat and stuff. Then I see it: her bulging belly. Don't get me wrong, I knew she was pregnant. It hadn't slipped my mind. Not after that awkward-as-hell phone interaction a while ago. But to see her here, in person, with this basketball shape under her blouse, that's a whole different ball game. She smiles and starts explaining why she's here, but I'm not listening. I'm checking out her face, which hasn't changed a bit. No, scratch that. She's, like, radiant with that baby inside her. They say some women do that. I had never seen it before, but there it is. Like a forty-watt under her skin. All for that little round bulge there between us. She hugs me, and I bump into it.

"How have you been?" she asks, all concerned like Fiona used to do. I don't want her freaking sympathy.

"Good," I say. "This is a surprise."

I meant her stopping by, but she's thinking something else. She rubs her belly and says, "I know. Quick, huh? Getting engaged after six months and then—whoops! And here we are!" She laughs and blushes a little.

"Yeah, that too."

Now she looks uncomfortable. She asks to sit. We both do, on separate sides of the living room.

"So, Fiona tells me you finished your book, and it's sold? That's amazing. I'm so happy for you."

"Actually, mine hasn't sold. Yet. The book we're here for is Jerry's. Well, ours I guess. It was kind of a joint effort." Our story sounds totally lame when I tell it to Teresa. Besides, I'd be mortified if she read it and knew it was *me*.

"Wow, so you're co-authors?"

"Well, not really. Jerry's the author…" I trail off. I really don't want to get into it.

"Hey, you know," she says. "I wanted to say, well. I wanted to talk to you about how things were left between us. I feel like you deserve a bit of an explanation."

I hold up my hand. "No need. Really, Teresa. It's cool." But even as I say it, my mind starts spinning the scene again.

I'd been surfing. I came home to our beach-side rental in San Diego, and there she was: sitting on the bed, crying—the steady, streaming kind. It was like she'd been in bed all day. The sheets and stuff were all messed up. And she still wore her nightgown. She hugged a pillow and looked up at me, her eyes bloodshot.

"What happened?" I asked her.

She shook her head. Nothing? I tried to coax her out of bed. But she wasn't having any of it. I had no idea why she was freaking out. I kept asking her what was wrong and she kept crying and shaking her head, not letting me hug her or anything.

Finally, she said, "It's this, Alden. I can't do it anymore. I can't live this way." Then she really broke down.

It was like someone hollowed out my ribs. "What do you mean? What way?"

"With you."

I nearly died of shock. For real? Just yesterday we were mashing on the pier at sunset. We talked about getting hitched. Just *yesterday*.

I started grasping at anything. "T, you don't mean that. Maybe you're tired. Were you up again last night?"

She shook her head.

"You can't mean…we're not breaking up. You can't mean that."

"We have to…" She could barely get the words out. "Alden, I have to. I have to go. I have to move back East."

"I'll go with you."

"No. You belong here."

"I belong with you. We belong together, T."

"No. We don't." This was it. Her words were final. Sober. Uncrying. That's when I knew it was for real.

Of course I tried. You got to know, I fought to keep her around, to save what we had. But then it all rolled out. She really stuck it to me: "You're not ready. You don't give me what I need. You're still a hippie. You think you've grown out of it, but you haven't. You don't *really* want to be married and have kids."

That just about killed me. After almost *two years*, she's going to tell me what I want and don't want?

But she was firm. She insisted. She cried her eyes out while she packed her suitcase. And then she was gone.

I'm all worked up thinking about it again, even though it's been well over a year. Now she's sitting with me in Fiona's living room, and I force myself to look at her without breaking down. I still feel like she's my girl. Can't I just take her hand? Wasn't it just yesterday when we mashed on the pier?

"Alden," she says, her eyes all teary. "You know I'll always love you."

I shake my head. Stop, I want to say. But there's a catch in my throat. Why is she doing this? She's about to have *someone else's* baby. What the hell would *he* think if he heard that?

She goes on. "I want to apologize if there was something I said that hurt you—"

I burst out with a laugh. Well, a cry-laugh. *One thing* you said? You said a lot of things. But it was more than what you *said*, sweetheart. You *left* me! But I can't talk. My throat's totally clogged. I turn away and study the fireplace so she doesn't see tears. Don't blink, Alden. Don't let her see you wipe your cheeks. Don't let her know. Eyes wide, Alden. Eyes wide. Goddam! I'm so pissed right now. I wish she would just go. I wish she never came here.

But she keeps talking. "I never meant that you weren't good enough, or smart enough, or ambitious enough. That wasn't it—"

"What was it, then?" This comes out all wrong. Mean. I regret saying it as soon as it's out. But then, it's out.

"I don't know anymore. Looking back, we probably could've worked it out."

What. The. Fuck. I can't *believe* she just said that!

"But I was scared, Alden." Her voice is all shaky now. "We were far away from my family and I was getting really wrapped up in our life out there in paradise and our laid-back lifestyle. It seemed too carefree. I don't know. I just got scared. It wasn't the picture I had in mind. For me. For my life."

I can do nothing but shake my head at her. And shrug. I think I shrug. Whatever. It doesn't matter. I don't give a hoot if she knows I'm crying now.

"I'm sorry, Alden," she says. "It was my fault. That's really all I wanted to say."

Big Dave comes in through the garage. He calls from the kitchen, "Someone here, Alden?"

"Hi, David!" Teresa calls, her voice strained.

He runs in, his boots still on, tracking in mud and crap. He looks at Teresa like she's broken in to rob the place. He was probably under strict orders to keep her away from here. Word, that's probably why he was outside to begin with. Awesome work, Big Dave. Way to save the day.

"It's okay," I tell him, because he's totally kicking himself inside, I can tell. I'm glad he's here, though. Gives me a second to chill the hell out.

"I was just going," Teresa says. Good thing too, before big Dave pushes her out the door.

We're all quiet while Teresa makes a big production about putting her coat on. It's like the baby makes it hard for her to move. I think about that little bulge bumping me when she hugged me earlier. And it's like something shifts in me. She's still Teresa and beautiful and extraordinary. She has the face I will always associate with love. But she belongs somewhere else, to someone else: that baby. A baby who has nothing to do with me.

And it's cool. I mean, I can learn to be cool with that.

I help her with her scarf and stuff.

"You're going to be an awesome mother," I say. And I mean it. For real.

"Thank you, Alden." She beams at me, and her eyes are green-gold from the light coming in. She takes my hand. It's as soft as I remember.

"You're going to be a wonderful author," she says.

Chapter 27
Jerry

If nothing else, the scenery is worth the trip. I'm driving David's Buick through the rolling hills of western Massachusetts. The Berkshires have shed their fall colors yet hold a clean purity as they await the first snowfall. The panorama out the windshield offers the kind of vista that makes you want to take a deep breath.

We're on our way back from the Amherst-Northampton area where we had gigs in some cool, independent bookstores where college kids hang out. This time I read the part where Holden goes on that date with Sally. I figured it would get a few laughs. And it did. And we sold a bunch of books, so it was an overall success.

If only I could get rid of that nagging pit in my stomach.

"It's really nice what you're doing," Kiki pipes up from the backseat, startling me. I had thought she was dozing back there. Fiona, who sits in the passenger side, shoots me a look.

"Sorry?" I ask. "Are you talking to me?"

"I know it must not be easy," Kiki says. "I know how angry Alden is. But you're seeing it through. It's the right thing to do."

I'm not sure what to make of this. "You think?"

"Alden will come around," she says. "You'll see. If you could see it from my eyes, you would see a pretty awesome family."

I catch Fiona smiling from the corner of my eye.

"Well, it's not without our challenges," Fiona says.

"That's what I mean," says Kiki. "Everyone has problems. Family stuff is always tricky. But even through this mess, you all are sticking by each other. It's inspiring."

Fiona inhales sharply. "Aren't you seeing your sister in New York, Kiki?"

"Yep," she says with a finality neither Fiona nor I wish to challenge. It's quiet after that. Soon, Kiki is stretched out in the backseat dozing for real.

I have to say, she's hit a nerve. Of course I'm seeing this through, despite how demeaning it's become for me. And if it brings Alden pain to revisit this time in his life, who am I to insist he participate in the tour? If it were possible—or if Fiona hadn't worked so hard—I'd cancel the whole thing.

Fiona interrupts my thoughts. "What did you think of that MD person?"

"Oh, he was great. I loved how he just put it to Heffernan."

"Right. He sure did have a lot of…energy in his enthusiasm. You should've seen him while you were out watching for David. He started laughing hysterically for no reason. It was borderline inappropriate. Don't you think that's odd?"

I chuckle. "Hey, the guy wears a fur hat. And he thinks Alden's teenage journal is more important than the work of John Keats. I think he's the very definition of odd."

"Right," Fiona says, and grows quiet, gazing out the window.

Alden's teenage journal. God, just saying those words makes it real again. Reminds me of what I did. I hope what Kiki says is true. I do hope Alden comes around. In as much as I hope he forgives me. I'm not sure what I can do besides apologize until I'm blue in the face, but I hope he is able to find forgiveness in his heart. I mean, if the tables were turned…

Oh my God.

It's just dawned on me. This whole ride, I've been sitting next to Fiona with that *thing* between us. My thing. My grudge about that review she did years ago. It's still there. I'm *still* mad at her.

Suddenly, it all becomes as clear as the early December sky. I glance at Fiona, poised to speak, only to find her looking at me with an eagerness all too familiar.

"Jerry," she says. "I have something to confess—"

No way. I refuse to torture my siblings any more. "Fiona, please. Let me. I have something to confess too." Deep breath. "Fiona, my sister…I have been angry with you for nearly ten years. You wrote that review about *The Boatnicks* and it really…bruised my ego. I mean, it was a really bad review. You'd have to agree. Scathing, actually. It was humiliating for me. I was so embarrassed my kid sister slammed me in my industry where I'd worked so hard to build a solid platform. It was like you smeared my name in a community you were just visiting for a while with your first job out of college—but I lived there. I was like, 'How dare that snotty little bitch! Who does she think she is?' I know; it was bad. I blamed you for not getting decent jobs after that, did you know that? But it probably was just luck of the draw. *Bad* luck of the draw. Who knows if anyone in LA even reads the movie reviews in the *Boston Globe*? Although it *was* in the Sunday paper..."

"Jerry, I—"

"Nope. Don't you dare apologize. It's my turn to apologize. I'm sorry for holding onto that anger for so long, and directing it toward you. You did nothing wrong. You did your job, giving an honest review. What else were you supposed to do? Play favorites? Refuse the job? Fiona, I am so, so sorry. Will you forgive me?"

Fiona blinks a few times. I'm sure she's surprised as hell to hear this from me. But I'm so glad it's out. God, it feels good—cathartic!—after holding onto that ugliness for so long. Gone. Done. What a relief!

"Um, okay." She takes a long drink from her bottle of Sprite.

It's quiet again, but the mood inside the car has lifted so much the air feels as light as the leafless trees we're speeding past. I feel like a new man. Wow, why didn't I think of this sooner? I'll have to thank Kiki at some point for making it clear. And I'll have to think of a way to get Alden to see that I am truly sorry. I'll have to do something. Some sort of penance. Taking over the tour is not enough. But I'm headed in the right direction. Damn, I feel like dancing. I'm tempted to turn on the radio, but maybe Fiona wants to talk some more.

"So, everything's cool?" I say, tapping her knee—an awkward attempt at affection.

"Sure. Yeah."

But her smile looks tentative, like there's something on her mind.

"So," I say. "When is Heffernan's article out? I can't wait to see how he tries to spin MD's outright praise of the book."

Fiona gulps more Sprite, and crosses her legs. Maybe she has to go to the bathroom? She looks downright uncomfortable. Could be the pregnancy, I guess.

"Right," she says. "Not sure. Maybe tomorrow we'll see the article. Yes, it will be interesting to read what he chooses to publish."

Chapter 28
Alden

It's Monday. On our way to New York City. Not sure what Fiona has in store in the Big Apple. But it's groovy to be on a train. Kiki's beside me, laughing at all my jokes. Jerry and Fiona are having their own love fest a few rows in front of us. Fiona keeps squealing about baby stuff and Jerry's full of phony comebacks. It's like, since the trip to western Mass, they're bosom buddies. Whatever.

Just a tad jittery to make an appearance in New York. I can count on my hand how many times I've checked it out since my big breakdown. That's why I'm a comic on the train, to take my mind off it. Would be cool to put the book out of my mind too. What a downer. So I keep telling stupid jokes. "What do you call a camel with no humps?"

Kiki, primo audience, is already laughing. "I don't know. What?"

Before I can say the punchline—*bam!*—the connecting door from the train car in front of us bursts open. Guess who walks in?

"No way!" I'm on my feet high-fiving MD before anyone else sees him. "If it isn't my favorite fan!"

"You're here!" MD says, his face glowing pure joy like a kid at Christmas. "I can't believe we're on the same train. Synchronicity. It's amazing."

"Word. Did you read that article in the *Globe*? You were quoted all over the place. It was stellar."

"No. I haven't seen it yet. Do you have a copy?"

"I don't, but Fiona does." I reach over and fluff my sister's hair. "Fiona? You got the Heffernan article? Look who's here. MD hasn't seen it yet."

Fiona glances at MD and looks away, awkward-like. She rummages through her tote bag, mumbling something. She hands the article to me without meeting my eye. For real, she makes a point to look *away* from us.

But MD grasps her hand. "Fiona," he says quietly. "My apologies for my outburst the other day. It was a completely inappropriate emotional response. I do that sometimes. You can ask my mother. I'll be at a funeral and start cracking up. Weird things get into my head when sad or serious things are supposed to be there. It's a shameful habit. More like a tic. I just can't help it. The world just doesn't make any sense sometimes."

"Oh, that's okay," Fiona says, taking her hand away. MD turns back to me, so he doesn't see her wiping her hand on her shirt.

"Let's go to the lounge for a cold beer," he says.

I smile broadly. "I'm game."

At the lounge, he orders us two Heinekens and then asks if they have chocolate mousse. That kills me.

"I like to have chocolate mousse when I travel," he explains. "It makes me feel fancy."

Dude is a riot. I'm cracking up.

Before I get the chance to show him the article, he reaches into his duffle bag and whips out the book. He flips to a page toward the end and reads: "*It was Monday and all, and pretty near Christmas, and all the stores were open.*"

I suck on my beer, not getting it. "Yeah?"

"Amazing," he mutters, as if to himself. "The coincidence is just amazing. Today is Monday. It's pretty near Christmas."

I shrug. "Sure, I guess that's cool."

"History and time," he says, nodding to emphasize his point. "Synchronicity."

"Yeah, whatever." I push the article to him. "Read this. It's killer."

"Killer?" He's smirking. When he reads he moves his lips like kids sometimes do. I crunch away on the complimentary pretzels while I wait. He's got a film of sweat working his upper lip by the time he's done. The newspaper shows soggy fingerprints where he held it. He clears his throat and folds the paper carefully. Doesn't say bunk, just puts it back on the counter.

"Pretty cool, huh?" I say.

He's daffed out, though, thinking about who-knows-what. When he gets to talking, it's barely above a whisper. "He didn't use my name."

"No, but all you said was in there. Like, verbatim."

"Right." He chuckles. "Who am I anyway? Just some dude that traveled all the way from Hawaii to get my book signed."

"And to meet John Lennon," I tease.

"Of course." His lips draw down around the bottle rim.

"Yeah, I was thinking about joining you. I've always wanted to meet him. He's, like, my hero."

He looks at me like I'm speaking Japanese. "Who?"

"John Lennon. Aren't you planning to get his autograph in New York? Isn't that why you're on this train?"

MD nods with his whole body. His face opens up with a huge grin. "Oh, yes! Yes, I think that's a perfect plan. You should come with me. You need to. That will be perfect."

"Cool. Let's do it."

MD lowers his voice, all secretive. "Do you know that Charles Manson's *Helter Skelter* killings were inspired by the Beatles—specifically *The White Album*? He thought there was some sort of message in the lyrics that signaled this, like, civil war among races and socio-economic groups."

I cough, kinda choke on my brew. "Manson is one sick dude."

MD gives me this zappy grin and pets the goddam book again, wiggling his eyebrows as if I'm in on some inside joke. Then he says it again: "Synchronicity."

"What gives, jive turkey?" I tease, shoving his shoulder. MD just laughs. I'm not even sure if I know what he means, but that's, like, the fiftieth time he's said that word: synchronicity. Whatever.

Neither of us talks for a bit. Just slug our brews. It's cool at first but then it's like he's totally wrapped up in his own thoughts, so I bring him back to earth.

"Yo, so how did you end up in Hawaii?"

He shifts on his stool. "Oh, well. Who wouldn't want to live among sunshine and rainbows every day?"

I raise my hand, give him my imp-grin. "I wouldn't. I think it would be depressing as hell. All that pressure to live like life is one big luau. It'd put me right in the funny farm."

"Right," he says, serious now. "Listen, Fiona clued me in about something. But she barely needed to. I know Jerry's name is listed as author, but when he does the readings, it's like he's reading someone else's words. It's not his voice, you know?"

Now I start to burn up. "Oh?"

"I know it says you're the inspiration, but it's more than that. These are your words, aren't they?"

I shrug. "Yo, I never wanted to publish the thing."

"I know," he says, nodding in that pointed way counselors do.

"It was all Jerry's idea." I try to recover. My fingers tremble around the bottle neck. "He was all hot to publish it. And he had the connections, so. He thought it would be a hit. And I guess it's doing pretty well. So far."

"It was not cool," MD says, his voice low and sharp with bitterness. "And it's ironical. Because he's like the people you describe in the book. He's the biggest phony of them all, selling himself as the author when he clearly is not."

"Never thought of that." I kinda regret talking about it. Jerry did a shitty thing, but it's between the two of us. MD's, like, taking it personally. "He's not a bad guy," I say. "Just made a mistake."

A bark of a laugh from MD. "I'll say! Pretty big one. What you say in this book, though, is so true. I think most people live their lives in a dishonest way. There are so many hypocrites out there. It's disgusting." He opens the book again. "You say it perfectly in that scene with

Spencer. He says, '*Life is a game, boy. Life is a game that one plays according to the rules.*' And Holden thinks: '*Game, my ass. Some game. If you get on the side where all the hot-shots are, then it's a game, all right— I'll admit that. But if you get on the other side, where there aren't any hot-shots, then what's a game about it? Nothing. No game.*'"

"Yeah, well. It's just a kid—"

"Right. And kids are the most honest beings on earth. And they are trusting. And they are naïve. And then they learn the hard way that they are surrounded by hypocrites."

"I don't know—"

"You know who the worst culprits are? Celebrities. All those rich and famous people. Especially the ones who think they are hippies—who think they stand for peace and love and simplicity. All that malarkey with bed-ins? It's a hoax. They sit in bed while interviewers come into their bedroom and their valet brings them five-course meals."

This sounds familiar. "Are you talking about John and Yoko?" I remember an article from a few years back with pictures of them lounging in their hotel bedroom with a homemade sign that read *Peace* over their headboard.

He takes a messy sip, dribbling beer down his chin. He points at me. "Exactly. Could there be a bigger hypocrite? He's the phoniest one of all. All those songs about love and peace, and he's sitting up there living like royalty."

"I guess."

"Exactly!" He opens the book and gets ready to read again. I'm not in the mood, though. I slide my empty to the bartender's station.

"Kiki probably thinks I'm a runaway." MD's immersed in the book, not listening. I give him a nudge. "Yo, it's just a book."

He turns to me, looking shocked and hurt. "It's a powerful book that holds many answers." He pets the cover. "Let's write chapter twenty-seven...together."

I laugh at that; the book has twenty-six chapters. There is no part two. Nor do I want there to be. But—whatever—this MD dude seems like he needs a little something to hold onto. He kinda reminds me of someone, maybe from school. A little troubled. "Sure, bro. Let's do it," I say with a shrug. I stand and stretch my legs. "So, I'll see you in New York?"

He half-smiles and does that slow nod again. "Absolutely. Do you know where Lennon lives? Let's make a plan to meet. Right in front of the Dakota."

Chapter 29
Fiona

How I wish David could've taken some time off work so he could be here with me. Such a beautiful day in New York City. There's a dreamy snow flurry in the air, the sun is playing peek-a-boo with clouds, and Christmas is everywhere. I'm on my way to meet Jerry at Ballard Books on the corner of 71st and Amsterdam—taking in the impressive Fifth Avenue window displays en route. We used to visit this bookstore as kids. I remember it had a big box of puppets at the back of the store. Alden would take me there and we'd act out my Hazle Weatherfield stories. He always had been a good sport about that kind of thing. He and Kiki are meeting her sister right now at a diner on the Upper East Side.

I also wish my mood matched the day. Alden's relinquished all involvement in the tour. Even my coaxing hasn't helped. Even worse, he's hardly speaking to Jerry—and he's glommed on to that strange MD person as if he were our own kin. I can't believe he ended up on our train! What if he purposely arranged his travel plans around us? What happens if he interferes with another interview or, worse, leaks Jerry's theft to a reporter? What then?

Distracted by my window tour, I arrive at Ballard Books later than I wanted—Jerry is already done with his reading and on to book signing. Shoot! And I'm not feeling so great. Now that I've stopped walking, my stomach feels like a ball of lead, like I'm already eight months along. I'm sweating profusely under my thick winter coat. My scarf feels like it's glued to my neck. I must look as bad as I feel because the store's owner, Shay, a California native with a wiry mass of grey hair, offers me her personal wooden stool from behind the counter. My throbbing feet are grateful.

At the back of the store, Jerry is sitting at a table surrounded by a small, polite crowd. It looks like a pretty good turnout, about a dozen people, although it's low for New York standards. He seems in good spirits; his eyes are calm and warm with appreciation. He chats good-naturedly with all the customers. I can't help but wish Alden were here.

Okay, to work. I consider what's on the docket for the rest of the week. This is the last reading; I hope Jerry didn't notice I was missing. Tomorrow we have an interview with Steve Oglowski from the *New York Post*. I've brought a copy of the *Globe* article to show him. Wait—I gave my copy to Alden. Who gave it to MD. Did he get it back? I'll have to check. I'm making notes in my notepad when someone taps my shoulder.

"*New York Post*, huh?" he says. "Another interview?"

My entire body tenses. "MD. This is a surprise. How did you know we were here?"

"Where's your brother?" he says, his eyes wide.

I gesture to Jerry with a grin, although I know whom he means. His affinity for Alden borders on unadulterated obsession. Alden is only encouraging him, spending all that time with him on the train. It's making me terribly anxious. I rub my stomach in exaggerated circles, hoping MD has some semblance of empathy.

It seems he does not.

"Not him." He moves closer and I feel encircled by him. "Where's Alden? He was supposed to meet me last night but never showed."

His eyes dart to the front door, then back to me. I change the subject. "Did you stay for the reading?"

"Yes. I liked this selection much better. It really spoke to me. That's me. I swear."

He wipes his mouth with his wrist bandage, and then (I can't believe he does it) he opens his book and reads aloud, projecting like he's got a bullhorn:

"'*I keep picturing all these little kids playing some game in this big field of rye and all. Thousands of little kids, and nobody's around—nobody big, I mean—except me. And I'm standing on the edge of some crazy cliff. What I have to do, I have to catch everybody if they start to go over the cliff—I mean if they're running and they don't look where they're going I have to come out from somewhere and catch them. That's all I do all day. I'd just be the catcher in the rye and all.*'"

Everyone in the store is looking our way now. I must be as red as Rudolph's nose. I hope for divine intervention, since MD is preparing to read another passage. Jerry and I meet eyes. He looks bemused, suppressing a laugh. Great, Jerry. Thanks a lot. The few beats of silence last for ages.

"Honestly, do you think you could tone it down a bit?" I say to MD in a low voice.

"Am I making you uncomfortable?" he asks.

"Listen, I know you love the book, and that's wonderful. I know you have all these grand ideas about how to promote it. I appreciate that, but I really think we can take it from here. You don't need to…accompany us on the tour or anything."

His eyes jump behind his glasses. "Oh, Fiona. I'm not going to let you down. Trust me. Just wait and see. It will happen and it will be huge." He squeezes the book to his chest. "But, right now, I need to find Alden. I need him for my mission. For the grand thing that I'm doing for the book."

"Oh, MD. Let me save you the time. Alden doesn't want anything to do with the book anymore. Or Jerry. He's off doing his own thing with Kiki."

"No, no, no. He and I have discussed it. It was his idea to come with me. He's going to help. We talked about it on the train."

I can't imagine Alden planning anything with MD for the book. There must be a misunderstanding. I try to be casual. "What did you and Alden discuss on the train?"

Something clicks and MD straightens up, almost panicked. "Where's your brother? Where's Alden? I have to find him."

"I don't know," I lie.

MD chews on his lip. Then, he suddenly laughs— echoes of the maniacal laugh from the Park Plaza. "I know where he is!" he says, and raps his knuckle on the book cover. "It's right here. He gave me a map. I know just how to find him."

In a flash, he is gone—squeaking out of the store in his orthopedic shoes.

The bookstore is pretty empty by now. Shay offers me a glass of water, but I'm too agitated to take a sip. MD saw my notes about our meeting with the *Post*, and I'm terrified he will interfere. And what on earth does he want to find Alden for? Maybe it's not too late. Maybe we can intercept him before he does any damage.

I rush to Jerry, who's signing unsold books for the window. I'm already putting my coat on when I urge him: "Jerry, we have to find Alden. Now! Let's go!"

Chapter 30
Alden

We're en route to Anton's Diner to meet Kristin. Kiki is, like, running. Totally disrupting my smoking pace. You should've seen her face when I told her we'd see Kristin this morning. Lit right up, for real. But then she got nervous as hell. Kept asking me what she should wear. That kills me about chicks. They get all worked up about clothes when dudes barely notice. But when she asked me about her hairdo, I just plain laughed. "Kiki, your hair looks exactly the same every day," I said. But when she dropped her smile, I added, "I dig it. Just the way it is. Curly and wild."

So we're almost there when Kiki asks me again how she looks. I tell her, like, ten times she looks awesome before she finally goes in. We check out the place, which is kinda dead considering it's a diner at 10 a.m. in New York. Beats me who I'm looking for, but I'm pretty sure she's not here yet.

"She's not here," Kiki says, and looks like she's about to cry.

"She's probably on her way. We're early. Let's order some coffee. You hungry?"

"I can't eat!" she snaps, as if I've asked her to kiss an elephant.

I order myself a sticky bun and a large coffee. Kiki orders ice water. Word, she's nervous. I try casual chitchat to relax her, but she's not listening. Her knee is jiggling so hard the table shakes. I give up and enjoy my breakfast.

Then it's like—*bam!*—in comes Kristin. Couldn't miss this gal. What a poofer! Like a cartoon character. She's wearing a multi-colored jumpsuit with flared legs—a matching multi-colored headband containing her large blonde hair. Ridiculous amount of make-up on her face. Maybe I do know about fashion, because this chick has totally missed the boat. Kiki shouldn't have worried. The sisters hug and squeal; the dichotomy is striking. Kristin is like a child next to Kiki, who towers over her and is about twice as wide. Like a linebacker next to an infant ballerina. Kiki introduces me and Kristin acts as if we're old pals. She orders a "coffee-extra-cream" across the place. They don't answer, but she's got a "coffee-extra-cream" in front of her lickety-split.

I enjoy my sticky bun, letting the ladies catch up. Turns out to be interesting, I kid you not.

"Jinkies! My own sissy is right here. Kyra, you bitch!" Kristin says playfully. "Why didn't you tell me you were moving to New York?"

"I'm not moving. I'm just visiting."

"Yeah, I heard about the book tour. But who wrote the book?" Kristin points to me.

I squirm until Kiki says, "Alden's brother. I brought you a copy. It's signed by the author."

The book comes out of Kiki's handbag. That totally throws me off. She's been carrying that thing around in her bag all day? I hope Kristin doesn't open it and start reading, like, now.

"I don't read," Kristin says, slapping the book away. "You know that!"

I stifle a laugh. What kind of ditz would admit that?

But Kiki looks crushed. "Well, it's been a while. I wasn't sure. And it is written by a friend of mine. I thought you might—"

"I don't give a care if Mick Jagger himself wrote a book. I ain't readin'." She lights up and blows smoke in Kiki's face. Not doggish or anything. Just clueless. Kiki blinks like mad and puts the book back in her bag. Fine with me.

"So, how have you been, Kristin?" Kiki says. "Are you still acting?"

"Auditioning, you mean? I wait tables and audition. That's about it. Leo thinks it's all a big joke. Tells me to peace out, go to college or somethin'. What-ever…but he may be right. Like, they all keep telling me to get thinner. Taller too. Like I can grow anymore? Yo Kyra, you would be bitchin'. You're totally the right height. But, like, you want to lose like *at least* forty pounds before you audition. Actually, I thought you were already on the audition route in Californ-i-yay. What *are* you doing out there, anyway?"

Despite the insult, Kiki is still smiling. "I work as a data clerk at an oncology clinic."

Kristin blows more smoke. The whole table is full of it. "What the joe-hell is onc-lology?"

"Oncology," Kiki gently corrects. "We treat cancer patients."

Judging by Kristin's reaction, Kiki could have said "we treat pterodactyls."

"What the joe-hell would you want to do *that* for? It's not like it would be any *fun*." Kristin folds out her cigarette and sips her coffee. Both chicks ignore me. Like I'm invisible. Then, Kristin pulls her lipstick from her bag. Paints her lips hot pink. The coffee cup is painted too after her next sip.

"Speaking of Californ-i-yay, d'ya have a rockin time with Mom and Dad?" Kristin asks.

A flicker of confusion crosses Kiki's eyes. "N-no," she says. "They don't know I'm here. I wasn't planning on going to the island."

"No, goon! In *Californ-i-yay*. They went out there like a month ago. You didn't see them?"

Kiki's face falls, the color draining. She doesn't get to answer before Kristin starts in again, totally out to lunch.

"They brought me a couple bottles from wine country. Leo and I drank it in like two seconds. But it was, like, delicious. We have some bitchin' parents, don't we Kyra? For sure, how would I survive here in New York without their help? On my bogus income? Is stuff expensive out in Cali? I bet it helps you too."

"What helps?" Whoa. Kiki's, like, almost crying.

But Kristin doesn't notice; she's suddenly talking to me. "What helps, she says." She shakes her head. "Homegirl doesn't know how lucky she is. Tell her, Alden. Tell her that most parents cut their kids off after they move out of the house. Right?"

"Right," I say, my eyes on Kiki.

Kristin checks her watch. "Yo Anton, can I get a to-go cup or somethin'?" she shouts across the room. Then to me: "I gotta skitty. Waitressing at Delaney's six blocks away. They want me to wear this gnarly green uniform. So I gotta change. Too bad you couldn't meet Leo. He's rad."

Kristin kinda hugs Kiki's shoulders, an absent gesture, and offers me an open-mouthed grin.

"You two be good out there in Californ-i-yay!" She swings her big pocketbook over her shoulder, clutches her to-go cup, and bounces out. Kiki doesn't even watch her go. She's full-on crying now, tears and everything. I slide in next to her and put my arm around her.

"Hey, it's okay. You were great. So sweet. I'm sure she loved seeing you."

Kiki shakes her head and says something. "No," I think. It sounds more like a generic sob.

My heart wants to break seeing her so sad. I kiss her all over her face, any place I can reach. I stroke her springy curls while I kiss her forehead, her cheek, her eyelids, her nose. I taste salty tears and it breaks me up, but I keep kissing her. I don't give a hoot if people are staring. But then she shocks me, starts giggling. I stop, and kinda hold my arms out. "What?" I say, a little annoyed.

"You're funny with all those kisses. I'm a big girl, Alden. I'll be fine."

Suddenly, a big ruckus comes through the door. It's Fiona and Jerry.

"What's the deal?" I ask. Fiona flops into a chair, out of breath. Kiki fetches her some water. Jerry puts his hand on my shoulder and kinda whispers, "It's MD. He's looking for you."

What the hell, Jerry? I want to sock him in the face, but I shrug off his hand instead.

206

After a long drink, Fiona waves me over. It would be rude to deny a pregnant chick, so I go. But I keep my eyes on Kiki.

"Alden," Fiona says. "MD's looking for you. We need to find him so we can stop him before he talks to our contact at the *Post*. He saw my notes."

"Word. He'll gush about it like he did for the *Globe*."

"No, it's more than that," Fiona says. "He's not only obsessed with the book, he's obsessed with finding *you*. It sounded like he had some sort of plan in mind. He said you were going to help him? Did you two plan something together on that train?"

"Oh, that. No biggie. I was going to try and get Lennon's autograph with him—"

"Alden, are you sure that was it? He seems to have something in mind about promoting the book. Did he mention anything about that?"

"Promoting the book? No. Word—just that he didn't think the article was…big enough. That's all he said about the book."

Fiona shakes her head. "Why is he so eager to find you, Alden?"

Maybe I had too much coffee because I get all jittery. "How am I supposed to know?"

Fiona looks so stressed out, so I try to mellow. "But, for real, he's trying to find me? Do you think that's possible? How is dude going to find me in the middle of New York? It's not like I'll be waiting at the end of a rainbow or anything."

Jerry holds up a copy of the goddam book. "That's not what he thinks."

Chapter 31
Jerry

My hunch is that MD is going to visit the landmarks described in the book in hopes to find Alden. So here we are on the subway—me and Alden—alone for the first time on this whole tour. We're searching for MD, who's searching for us. Quite the circuitous pickle.

Yet, this feels like penance. Alden still won't speak to me, yet. But I know how he thinks; I know how to change his mind. If Fiona is right and MD has something up his sleeve, I'm going to be the one to stop it.

At the coffee shop Fiona stressed we had to get to him before he got to the *Post*. "The last thing we need is a bunch of drama around this thing."

Alden huffed, still pissed as hell. He hadn't wanted to leave Kiki, but Fiona promised to get her safely back to the hotel and insisted we go. You can't very well refuse a pregnant gal.

As the subway car rocks through a few stops, I skim the first few chapters of the book. I should have this shit memorized by now. Where did Alden go on that three-day journey through NYC? But then the answer is right there.

I call to Alden, "So, first Agerstown, I guess."

Alden is staring at the blur of concrete out the window of the moving train. He talks to it, not me. "No way in hell are we going to Pennsylvania, Jerry. I know where he is."

I'm definitely not going to argue with the guy. I skim ahead a few chapters, get past the train scenes. "I guess the Edmont, then."

Alden says nothing, just taps the subway pole—a nervous reflex. I feel like a kid in trouble, waiting for my parents to dole out a punishment. Forget that. I'm taking control. I stand to meet Alden's eyes. "Alden, please tell me what you and MD talked about on the train?"

Alden runs his fingers through his mop of hair, eyes me suspiciously—like he's weighing his options. "I don't know what Fiona is so worked up about. Besides her own slip—" The train stops, interrupting him. People shuffle on and off, jostling us closer together. "It's a goddam ant farm," he says under his breath, huddling against the pole. "All of New York is a goddam ant farm."

The train sways back in motion. "You said Fiona slipped?" I ask. "What do you mean?"

"She told him the truth. Or confirmed it. About how you stole my journal. Published it behind my back. He knows it all."

"Oh, shit."

Alden's words nag like Monday morning's alarm clock: *...you stole my journal...published it behind my back.* Not only do these words prove I'm an asshole, but now this MD guy knows it. I stare down at the book in my hands, my name screaming off the cover in bold, Times New Roman. On the back cover is a photo of me. I'm leaning against a tree, grinning smugly with my arms folded. You know who I see in that photo? A prick who should get what he deserves, even if it's delivered by some overzealous fan. I can picture it all unraveling: an image of me flashes on the screen, my hand blocking the camera, the caption scrolling: *Who's the real author?*

This fucking book. Measly. Insignificant. And yet—it's spurred all this bullshit. I should burn every last one of them.

I turn back to the cover to hide my face—from Alden especially.

Alden eyes me through slits. "MD doesn't care about you. Waste of time."

I shove the book under my arm. "So, his plan is to…?"

"He's still zappy for the book. Maybe he doesn't care how it got published. Fiona's worried he's going to leak it to the press. Your plagiarism. But he wouldn't need my help for that."

"What would he need your help with?"

Alden shrugs. "The only thing that came up on the train…the only plan we talked about was getting John Lennon's autograph."

"What does that have to do with the book?"

His eyes flicker to the map above the doors as the train slows down. "Next stop is ours," he says.

Like a shot, Alden is on the platform, and then bounds up the stairs two at a time. As soon as we come into daylight, he lights up a cigarette. It hits me: daylight. Damn! I pound the book with my fist and catch up to Alden.

"This isn't going to work, Alden. It's the middle of the day."

He keeps walking. I wave the book in his line of vision.

"Alden, this all takes place at night. In the *middle* of the night. It makes no sense to go to the Edmont now. The damn Lavender Room won't even be open."

He stops, sucks on his cigarette, staring at the traffic. It seems colder here, more windy. I'm shivering, waiting for him. I almost ask him for a cigarette just to warm my hands, but—

"We're not going to the goddam Edmont." And he picks up his absurdly fast pace again. I work my stride into a jog, wishing I had a hat. The kind with flaps on the sides to keep my ears warm. I smile inwardly, remembering the kid in the book like he's an old buddy. I look at Alden weaving his lanky body through the sparse crowd. His hair is an uncombed mop, and his worn jacket falls at the hip of his ripped jeans. He looks like a big kid. But laugh lines are hidden beneath his scruff, and his eyes have a depth and an honesty reserved for Buddhist monks or tribal elders, reminding me what I already know: This kid has been through something. Nothing is more important than protecting him now, my little brother. I have to make things right.

The sounds of the city are quieted as we enter the sanctuary of Central Park.

"Aha! We're going to see the ducks. You're right, Alden. That's what happens first in your journal. Central Park is the first stop in New York, really. I'll bet he's there for the ducks. It's worth a try, anyway."

"Are the ducks really there?" Alden says, stamping out his smoke. "It's, like, cold out."

"Oh, we're not starting this, are we?" I say.

"What?" he asks.

"You're telling me you don't remember that part?" I can't help but grin.

"No." He seems genuinely confused. "Central Park is not our destination. We're just cutting through. The Dakota is—"

He stops dead in his tracks, his eyes locked on something.

From this vantage point, we can see most of the pond. It takes me a moment, but I see him. MD. I can't believe we found him! Even though I should feel lucky—finding him was the whole point—I only notice how eerie everything is. Years in the military teach you to distrust luck. MD's throwing crackers or bread to the ducks, who are indeed here despite the cold. Huh. All those years, my whole childhood in New York, I never gave the ducks much thought.

"Aha," Alden says.

I grab his arm. "Wait."

He looks back, confused, but then he rips his arm away. "What, Jerry? What are you telling me to wait for?"

"I mean, what are you going to say to him? He's obviously not waiting around for an autograph. He's feeding the ducks. I'm no marketing genius, but I'll bet that his idea to promote the book does not include the damn ducks."

Alden looks as if he might burst. "I don't know what I'm going to say to him. Just confab. Who knows? But I have to go. Fiona was all twitchy about it. What—you want to go back and tell her we saw him but he was only feeding the ducks?"

"Alden, MD came here to find *you*. Why does he want to find you?"

"The fuck do I know! He's all gaga for the goddam book. To hear him talk about it, you'd think it's God's word or something. He knows you stole it. He knows you're a big phony…and he hates phony people more than Holden does."

I hold my breath, taking this in. I'm not sure I follow. "But, why would he want to find you—"

"You know what I think?" Alden gives me a crooked smile.

"What?"

"I think you're stalling because you're chicken. You can't handle confrontation. So just leave it all to me. I'll find out what's he's planning, if anything, and I'll go and make Fiona feel better. And you can just glide along like you've done the whole time."

What the *hell*. "Glide along? I'm trying to make things right—"

"Just chill, Jerr. Just stay away from me."

I remain still, stung. I can't help it. Alden saunters to where MD is still feeding those stupid ducks, moving in on him, his pace slow, normal, casual—he doesn't even disturb the ducks. He's got one hand in his pocket, the other waving friendly-like. He calls, "Yo, MD!"

I watch him walk down, my body heat rising with shame, wishing I were a bigger person. Wishing I were more like my brother.

Chapter 32
Alden

So what does MD do when he finally hears me calling him? He peels out. Runs like a goddam wild turkey. His trench coat is open and fluffs out like wings. He's carrying a decent sized duffle bag that makes him lean to his side a little. This is one dude who's not used to running, by the way. I run the hell after him. Now that I've found the zappy bastard, I'm not about to lose him. I'm like a magnet on him, wondering what the hell stupid thing is on his mind. Why the hell is he running from me?

I finally catch up to him and call his name, like, another hundred times before he stops.

"Alden?" he says, like he can't believe it.

"Who the hell did you think it was?"

"Alden!" His eyes get as wide as his huge glasses. "I'm so glad I found you. I have the answer. Well, I don't have the answer, but I know who does."

I take advantage of him being winded and move in closer. He's bending over like he's going to ralph, but he's just catching his breath. "What answer?" I say. "I don't copy."

"Ducks, Alden. Ducks." His breath is big, steamy puffs. "He knows where they go in the winter. We can finally find out."

What's with the ducks? "It *is* winter, MD."

"Not real winter. It's early December in New York! Winter's just getting started. Come on. Let's get to the Dakota."

MD takes off again at a slow jog. I'm right with him. And it's not because I want to find out where the goddam ducks go in winter. My stomach is all jacked up and adrenaline is pumping my legs. Even with all my smoking, I can outrun this dude. Before we're even out of the park, he's winded again. He slows and pops a squat on a park bench. Cool by me. I want to get to the bottom of this.

"MD, tell me something. What do you want to find John Lennon for? It's not about the goddam ducks, am I right? Does it have anything to do with the book?"

He's gasping for air, but that doesn't stop him from laughing at my question. "I told you I wanted to meet him. I told you I had two reasons for coming to the Northeast…"

"Word. I know. But Fiona has this wild idea that you and I planned some big promotional stunt. For the book. But all we talked about was getting an autograph. That's all we're doing, right?"

A few beats pass. "Let me ask you a question, Alden. Are you a Beatles fan?"

My turn to laugh. "Biggest fan there is. I have every album."

"What about this one?" From his duffle bag, he takes out an album. Far out! It's *Double Fantasy*, Lennon's solo album that just came out.

"Sweet! I actually don't have that one yet." I go to take it from him to look at, but he holds fast to it, and I pull my hand back. Whatever.

"Technically, it's not the Beatles." MD kinda caresses the images of Lennon and Yoko on the cover as if they're his long-lost friends.

"So," I say, trying to figure out what's going on. "That's, uh, what you want him to sign?"

"Well, sure!" he says, like a little boy. "What do you have?"

"Word." I pull out my half-empty pack of Marlboros. "This'll do. Let's boogie. Get some autographs."

I'm almost relieved. What I figure is this: If he's going to pull anything, like call Lennon a big phony and wave the book in front of TV cameras while at it, I'll be there to intercede, pull him back—this big marshmallow of a dude in his furry Russian hat and his dorky orthopedic shoes…he might embarrass himself but I tell ya, dude couldn't hurt a fly.

As we walk together at a regular pace, I feel chill enough to confab. "What do you do for work?"

"I've had a hodge-podge of careers," he says with a sigh. "My favorite job was as a YMCA counselor. Kids would call me Captain Nemo. My boss said I was like the Pied Piper. All the kids following me around, doing whatever I said, like I was really somebody. Somebody important. It was amazing. But that was in Georgia. Can't be a Y counselor forever."

"So, what do you do in the sunshine and rainbows?"

"I'm not working at the moment. I'm a house-husband, like Lennon. My wife is a travel agent. I've had my share of jobs, though. Most recently, I was a guard at a swanky apartment complex. Before that, I worked at a hospital…a mental clinic actually."

I almost trip. "What? How d'you get into that?"

"Used to be a patient." He gives me a mischievous grin.

"Get outta town. You jivin'?"

"I would not jive you, brotha."

I'm cracking up. "Why would you ever want to work there? As a former patient myself, you couldn't pay me enough dough to waste another second of my life in that joint."

He nods, rubs his chin—not offended in the slightest. He's quite the amiable dude. "Good point. But there were some decent people there. It sort of fell into place for me. Seems like life goes like that."

"Here's to coming through," I say, priming a high-five. "Even if it's got nothing to do with meds or therapy."

He obliges me with a weak slap. I can't believe I'm thinking it, but maybe MD was right. Maybe we are linked in some way. Allie would know. It would be unspoken and intuitive and spiritual, and Allie would see it as clear as I see pigeon shit on 72nd Street. I picture his goofy, freckled face and that bright red hair. I smile to myself, feeling a boost. There must be a connection here; Allie must be here, putting us together and letting fate handle the rest. Word.

We round the corner and the Dakota is in sight. It's this old-world building with spires and arched windows—smack in the middle of New York. Like a great aunt of skyscrapers came to visit all her young, contemporary tower-nephews.

"Hmm, there are usually a few people milling around this entrance," MD says. "I think we probably have some time for lunch."

We cross the street to the Dakota Grill and get a window table to keep watch on the entrance. We order hamburgers and Heinekens.

"So," I say. "What does your wife think of this crazy adventure of yours?"

Something crosses his face. "What crazy adventure?"

"I mean, coming all this way for no big reason."

MD doesn't answer my question. He's staring at the Dakota, but there's an absence in his eyes, unfocused.

"I don't listen to Lennon or the Beatles all that much anymore," he says, talking super-fast. "Have you ever listened to Todd Rundgren? I'm all about his album *Deface the Music*. Sheer genius."

"I know that album. Isn't it, like, a parody of the Beatles? Not really rock music, is it?"

MD gets all red in the face and raises his voice. "You know, I'm sick of hearing how much the Beatles revolutionized rock music. Even if they did, so what? It doesn't make them gods! Oh, and how about when Lennon said the Beatles were more popular than Jesus? Who does he think he is, saying these things about God and heaven and the Beatles? It's blasphemy!"

MD's all worked up, spit flying out of his mouth. I'd be offended, but it's like he's not even talking to me, or anyone. He's just going off.

"He didn't mean it like that," I say. "He's an artist. He's expressive."

Waitress delivers the goods. MD calms down and we eat in silence. A small crowd gathers in front of the Dakota, probably there for autographs too.

"Ever been to the Statue of Liberty, Alden?" he says in this breathy voice.

"Sure."

"I had a thought yesterday of climbing to the top and jumping off."

I chew my burger real quiet.

He goes on: "I think I have some problems, and I don't know what some of them are. Every once in a while I think about doing it. Tried it once with my car in the garage. Obviously it didn't work. You ever try it?"

I shake my head, just barely. My hamburger is hard going down. Then MD does a funny thing: closes his eyes, and his lips start moving. He's not even whispering, but he's, like, talking inside himself. I outright stare at the zappy bastard. But when his eyes pop open, I nearly jump. He shakes his head, like trying to right his brain, and rummages through his duffle bag. Next thing I know, he's got the book open on the table.

He reads from a page toward the end: "'*This fall I think you're riding for—it's a special kind of fall, a horrible kind. The man falling isn't permitted to feel or hear himself hit bottom. He just keeps falling and falling. The whole arrangement's designed for men who, at some time or other in their lives, were looking for something their own environment couldn't supply them with. Or they thought their own environment couldn't supply them with. So they gave up looking.*'"

He closes the book and takes another bite of his hamburger. I know the context of that passage, and it's not comfy. It was, like, the pinnacle of my anxiety—hearing these words from my most favorite teacher. How he thought I was letting myself fall into a hole—a hopeless, endless pit with no one to blame but myself. I swig my brew. I'm not letting MD in on this one. This is not about me anymore.

"So," I say. "That's how you imagine falling off the Statue of Liberty?"

He tilts his head at me. "It is not by chance we met, you know. It's all coming together. I'm not afraid anymore. I don't feel that way. It's all about to change. I'm going to be somebody. It's like all this time I've been searching—and your book has helped me find myself. And here you are, with me, by my side. Synchronicity. It's amazing."

"What do you mean? Yeah, I'm right here, but geez, MD, what gives?"

He straightens up right-quick, wearing a grin as big as his wide face. "I told you, brotha! I want to meet John Lennon! I want an autograph!" He's on his feet. "It's time. Quick. Let's go." He throws a few bills on the table, grabs his duffle bag, and peels out. I'm right behind him.

We're outside the Dakota now with all the other Beatles fans. There's all this buzz about John and Yoko coming down soon. All this madness aside, I can't believe I'm really going to meet John Lennon. For real. I can't help but get totally stoked.

We're out there for a while. The sun comes out, warming up the sidewalk. It's like the Dakota exudes a heat of its own and everyone gathered round is feeling groovy. MD's smiling like a kid on a carousel. He's got his *Double Fantasy* album ready, holding it out even though John and Yoko are nowhere to be seen...yet. Then he breaks into song, rather loudly. Word. I know it's another loony thing he does, but in a way it's cool. Before you know it everyone else is chiming in, singing along. Even me.

Imagine no possessions
I wonder if you can
No need for greed or hunger
A brotherhood of man

Imagine all the people sharing all the world
You may say I'm a dreamer, but I'm not the only one
I hope someday you'll join us
And the world will be as one

MD mixes up some of the lyrics. I hear only part of his flub: *Imagine John Lennon...*

It's hard to hear any one person, though, since there's a group of about fifteen people or so singing. Very cool. MD is totally focused on getting Lennon's autograph. He goes to the sentry and asks the doorman, "Hi José, any word on when John and Yoko might be down? Or are they out?"

The doorman winks and shakes his head. "Mark, you know I can't tell you that, now. I have no idea if he even lives in this building."

"Yeah, okay, José," MD says, grinning like a co-conspirator.

"What—are you some sort of special guest?" I tease, shocked he's on a first-name basis with the doorman.

"José says there are a couple ladies who are here so often, John and Yoko greet them by name. Imagine that?"

We wait for what seems like another hour. I go through another half-dozen cigarettes. My feet are killing me. I'd been laughing about his dorky orthopedic shoes, but I'll bet they're super-comfy right about now.

Then I see him. I can't believe he's here.

No, not Lennon.

Jerry.

He's on the other side of the circle. He must've trailed us the whole time. What a pansy. MD doesn't copy that my brother is here. That's cool by me. Jerry's staring at me with that pitiful, concerned look Fiona used to give me, like I can't possibly take care of myself.

He waves me over. No, thank you. I lean down to MD. "Yo, I'm gonna split. I'll catch ya later."

"What? You're leaving? You can't leave. We haven't seen Lennon yet."

"Yeah, but my feet are toast. Maybe I'll come back."

MD's voice rises to desperate levels. "But what if you miss him? Suppose you don't see him again? Suppose he...goes to Spain or something? Suppose something happens to him?"

"Spain?" I laugh. "Dude, it's okay. Kiki's probably worried. Fiona too. Maybe I'll come back later."

"Yes! You have to come back. *Please*. Please come back."

He makes me shake on it. "I'll wait for you, then," he says.

"No way, dude. If you see Lennon, get his autograph. Don't wait for me."

He nods, but looks stressed out. I head toward Central Park. Jerry, unfortunately, catches up to me. "Hey, what'dya find out?" he asks.

"Nothing." My words are clipped. "Don't worry about it."

"Alden, don't tell me not to worry about it," Jerry says, the whiner. "I'm going to worry about it."

He grabs my arm and kinda stands in front of me. I give him my blank stare.

"Hey," he says. "I'm part of this too."

Jump back! That makes me laugh. What a bogus comment. Jerry totally gets it, too. But when I walk away, he stays right with me. I stop short.

"Yo, Jerr, I know you're my brother and all. You'll always be my brother. I suppose I should forgive you and move on. I suppose I could too if you weren't such a royal jackass."

"Alden, please—"

"Please what, Jerr? What the hell is all this? What am I doing chasing furry hat dude around New York City to see what big thing he might pull in hopes to sell the goddam book?"

"I know. I—"

"You know how it happened, Jerr? You got selfish. Greedy." Despite my attempt at self-control, despite my pacifist nature, I start to lose it. My voice is on the rise. I stab the air with my finger. "Did ya think about anyone else in all this? Did ya think you might hurt somebody?

Did ya think you might hurt *me*? Goddam you, Jerry. What are you trying to do to me?"

"Alden, I know. I regret the moment I—"

"I didn't want it out there!" I'm yelling at the top of my lungs. Tears are creeping down my face, which pisses me off even more. Jerry's standing there, palms out. Pathetic yellow bastard.

I can't stand it anymore. I tackle him. Take him down. We're rolling on the grass of Central Park, looking like a pair of stupid goons. I keep repeating, "Goddam you, Jerry!" We somehow get to our feet and Jerry pushes me away, but conciliatory-like. That gets me too. I throw some punches at his midsection. Although Jerry blocks me pretty well, he does not strike me. Not once. I throw a jab and a hook, neither land well. I end up tweaking my wrist. Fuck!

Finally, I just sit on a patch of dirt holding my goddam wrist in my lap while I mop my face with the other hand.

"Goddam you," I say, but I'm out of fight.

Jerry sits next to me. You'd think there'd be a crowd around us, but all the New Yorkers just go about their business. "Alden," Jerry says gently. "I want to make this right. Let me help. What can I do?"

I just shake my head and sniff like mad. Goddam Jerry. He's killing me.

But Jerry keeps talking. "What did you find out, Alden? Should we go back there?"

"Nutbag MD isn't going to do anything but get a freaking autograph. He is an odd dude. The kind that gets fixated on something. Just like he was fixated on getting the book signed, he's fixated on getting his album signed."

Jerry gives me a half smile, relief in his eyes. "Are you sure?"

I laugh aloud, the release irresistible. "There's no promotional thing. It's all about an autograph. He just wants Lennon's autograph."

Chapter 33
Fiona

I must have slept for nearly three hours; it's after five and my hotel room is dark when my phone rings. It's Kiki. We're to meet the guys for dinner at a new restaurant on 86th called Chartreuse, in an hour. Just enough time to shower and call David. But first, I want to confirm tomorrow's interview at the *Post*.

Steve Oglowski picks up after the first ring. "We're going to have to cancel that interview," he says when I try to confirm.

"Cancel? Oh. Perhaps we can reschedule."

"Listen, I wasted too much time on this already. I have to fill the Arts section with legitimate articles. I'm not going to entertain someone's dream to get fifteen minutes of fame. Not on my clock."

"I'm sorry. I don't follow—"

"Gentleman called yesterday claiming to be the author. Spent twenty minutes interviewing him when he switched his identity to the main character of the book. It was like talking to Sybil. He said he was part of your group, told me some scandalous info about how the book came to publication..."

Bile rises in my throat—and it has nothing to do with pregnancy. It happened. MD leaked it to the press. This is a disaster.

"Mr. Oglowski, please. This man is not in any way connected to the book other than the fact that he happens to be a huge fan. I'm not sure what he was trying to—"

"So you know him? The guy who called?"

I hesitate. "Unfortunately, yes. But he has no authority to speak on behalf of the book. Absolutely none."

"That's probably best, Miss. He didn't do you any favors. His story was convoluted and scattered. When he invited me to the Dakota with him, that's when I hung up."

"He invited you to the Dakota? Whatever for?"

"That's what I'm saying. It was scattered. He said he had a bigger story for me, but wouldn't give any details."

"Mr. Oglowski, my apologies for the confusion. I can assure you—"

"As I said, I've wasted too much time already. That's it, I'm afraid. I'm on deadline and I've got to go. Good luck to you."

Click.

My hands are shaking as I dial home. My concerns about what MD has done come out jumbled. David tries to reassure me. "Fiona, this is a book tour. He is a *fan* of the book. This is what you want. He's creating a buzz, right?"

"Believe me, he is not helping our cause! He called the *Post* and diverted our interview. He claimed to be the author, for goodness sakes!"

David chuckles. "Oh, boy. He didn't try that with me."

My stomach drops. "What do you mean?"

"He...called here. I thought you gave him our number? Anyway, we had a chat. He seemed like a nice enough guy. Yeah, he's in love with that book. But his affections seem to have shifted. He's into the celebrity thing now."

"I can't believe you spoke to him." I don't know if I'm disappointed or angry, but I'm absolutely shocked.

"I didn't think it was a big deal. I really thought you gave him our number."

"I didn't."

"I know that now."

It's like we're on completely different wavelengths. It's too much. I steady my voice.

"David, why did he call our house?"

A few beats pass. I can feel David's face fall. "He, um, well…he wanted to know where you guys were staying."

"And you told him?"

"Gosh," he says, sounding almost irritated. "Have some faith in me. I wouldn't tell him where you're staying. I know you don't feel comfortable around him. I discouraged him anyway."

"What do you mean, 'anyway'? Discouraged him from what?"

"He just said he needed Alden's help with something. That Holden's message is clear."

"What does that even mean?"

"That's what I'm saying. The whole thing was just confusing."

For a moment, I'm lost for words. Until I nearly boil over in anger. "David! Why didn't you call to tell me this? This is not normal—calling around like this. Inserting himself into our lives. Nothing good can come of this."

"Sorry, hon. I didn't think—"

"What did he need help with? Did he mention the Dakota?" I'm panicking now. "What did he want with Alden?"

David stammers, which is so unlike him. "That—he didn't say."

"Good work." Sarcasm is not me. But I can't help it. I'm realizing how hard it is to talk to David by phone, when I can't see his blue eyes reach over his wire-rims like an empathic professor. He's too quiet. And without the nonverbal communication, I'm lost.

After a long silence, David says, "I'm sorry, Fiona. I did try the hotel, but didn't leave a message."

"You know what he said to me on the train? That he reacts improperly in certain situations. Laughing during funerals. That sort of thing. He said he can't control his emotional impulses."

"He said that?"

"Something to that effect."

"He's probably just one of the millions who need psychological help." And with that, for David, it's over—he's sent him away with a diagnosis. It isn't until after we've hung up and I'm checking myself over in the bathroom, preparing to get to Alden and discover whatever stunt MD has planned, that I realize David didn't ask about the baby. I put a hand on my stomach that doesn't feel like mine anymore, and I want to weep. No one told me pregnancy could feel lonely.

Alden and Jerry are already at a table when we get to Chartreuse. I'm relieved to see my brothers laughing together. I let Kiki sit next to Alden, and I settle into a chair next to Jerry.

"Please tell me you've gotten to the bottom of it," I say to Alden. "Please tell me I don't have to worry about MD wreaking any more havoc on our family's reputation."

But he's busy tending to Kiki, and despite myself I'm touched. He rubs her back and whispers in her ear. She gives him a blushing smile and I notice her dimples.

He finally says, "Let me just get a drink first. A stiff drink."

Everyone orders rum and Coke and I have club soda. They bring out bread and butter and it's like they've thrown a doe to wolves. The basket is empty in minutes. Then the waitress takes our orders: steaks all around, salmon for me.

"Now I know why he wears that funny furry hat," Jerry says. "Considering all that time he's spent outside."

"You did find him, then?" I say to Alden. "How on earth…?"

"He was following the path set out in the book," Jerry says. "All the New York landmarks that were mentioned in the book…the stops Alden made way back when."

"Everyone's all hung up about the goddam ducks," Alden says with a mock sneer.

Jerry shoves him playfully. "Only because *you* were, brother!"

Maybe it's because I'm not drinking, but my anxiety grows the jollier they sound.

"You know he called the *Post* and posed as the author?" I ask. "And then he called *my house*? David spoke to him. He was trying to find you."

"Well, we all know this dude has a loose light bulb," Alden says.

"You should've seen him run like a bandit when Alden first found him," says Jerry. Both of them laugh.

"Why would he run?" I ask.

"Word!" says Alden. "Then he buys me lunch and we confab. Turns out—"

"He just wanted John Lennon's autograph," Jerry interjects.

"Zappy for an autograph," Alden says, waving his hands near his ears. "He's still there, hanging out by the front door. Lennon and Yoko aren't even there. Probably won't be for hours. But he's just hanging out there."

The guys and Kiki share a laugh, but I fail to see the humor. There's a missing piece of information. "Wait," I say. "Alden, what about promoting the book? What did he say he was going to do to promote the book?"

"Fiona, he's not," Alden says as our entrées arrive, a hint of irritation in his voice. "He just wants an autograph."

I shake my head. "It doesn't make sense, Alden. Why would he want *you* to be there to *help* him if all he wanted to do was get an autograph? There's got to be more to it. What connection does Lennon have to the book? There's got to be something in his bizarre mind that's linked the two."

Alden washes down steak with his cocktail. "Oh, he's kinda fixated on Lennon. As if the book refers to Lennon whenever the word 'phony' appears—which it does, like, a bunch of times. He's thinks Lennon is king of phonies with his songs about love and peace, while Jesus-bashing and living in the lap of luxury." He swallows and adds, "So, I guess that's the connection."

We all stare at Alden, who is now the only one eating.

"You didn't tell me that, Alden," says Jerry.

Alden looks up, his next bite primed at his lips. "What? It's no big deal, guys. He has a wicked *personal* interpretation of the book. Which is bogus, right? Because it's *my* journal...or was. And here's this guy who feels like it's him. And it's making him as confused as I was back then."

I cover Alden's hand with my own. "Why would he be so desperate for an autograph if he thinks Lennon is such a phony? Why would he go to the trouble? Are you sure he wouldn't be planning something else?"

"Like what?"

I fold my hands in my lap to stop them from trembling. "Alden, I don't know. But I have a bad feeling. Blame me or blame my hormones, but I think you need to go back there and make sure he doesn't do anything foolish."

"What could he possibly do?"

"I don't know! You hear stories in the news all the time about crazy fans who turn against their beloved idols...throw acid in their faces, or cut their hair off, or burn down their homes..."

Jerry gives me a confused look, but Alden seems to be losing color in his face.

"Alden?" Kiki says. "Are you okay?"

I force a breath and glance at Kiki, who—until now—hasn't said a word. Jerry and Alden take synchronized bites of steak and I'm left to wait until they finish chewing. Darn table manners. Alden and Jerry exchange a look I can't quite interpret.

"Alden, what is it?" I ask. "Do you think he might do something like that? Something to hurt Lennon?"

I can tell he doesn't want it to be true. He holds my gaze and I see a realization surface. He clamps his jaw and puts down his utensils. He tries a sip of water, but his hands are shaking.

He glances at his watch. "I think I should split."

"Where? Back to the Dakota?" Jerry says, his cheek bulging with steak.

"Go," says Kiki. "I'll go with you."

"No, Kiki, you stay," says Jerry. "Finish your dinner. I'll go."

"We'll all go," I say, pressing my napkin to the table.

"Stop it," Alden says. He feigns serenity as he saws off a hunk of meat. He doesn't take the bite, though. "I'm sure it's bunk. But I have whatever relationship with the dude, so I'm going alone."

Jerry wipes a napkin across his mouth. "No way, brother. I'm in this to the end."

Alden and Jerry nod to each other.

"Let's groove, then," Alden says. "You ladies go back to the hotel—"

"Don't tell us to rest, Alden," says Kiki, bless her heart. "We might go back to the hotel, but we will not rest until you boys are back safe and sound."

Alden smiles at her with affection. They're gone in a flurry, and I'm torn between relief and fear. I'm sure Kiki feels the same way, but she gives an honorable attempt at lightening the mood.

"Those bastards left us with the bill," she says, forcing a frown.

I take the slip of paper and grasp her hand. "Kiki, I'm so glad you're here."

Chapter 34
Jerry

Since when did Alden get such long legs? He's the smoker, and I've been busting my ass trying to keep up with him all day. He's even more edgy now than he was earlier. He can barely hold onto his cigarette.

"Alden, what do you think? Do you really think he might do something stupid?" I ask.

Alden talks so low I have to get closer to him. I make out only two words: *security guard*. When I ask again, Alden's expression is dark. "He used to be a security guard. Told me today. I can't dismiss the idea that he might have…" He mumbles the rest.

"Might have what?" I ask, exasperated and winded.

He mumbles again. "Alden, I can't hear you. Might have what?"

Alden slows down, stops. He looks utterly defeated. "A gun or something."

My stomach drops. I wipe my hand across my mouth, still catching my breath.

"Do you really think he'd use it, though? This is *John Lennon* we're talking about."

Alden begins to run again, and I have no choice but to follow.

"It doesn't make sense, Alden. He's a fan, right? Isn't that what he kept saying?"

Most people have a listening face at a book reading. You know, a slightly wrinkled brow, pursed lips. At the first reading in Boston I'd fantasized Janine was in the audience, blending in with everyone else. It felt good to imagine her out there, and I surprised myself by thinking how normal that would feel. To have her support. Her friendship. That's all. Maybe she'd have a listening face, but also a twinkle in her eye, like when she'd win an argument. I could picture it so clearly—and it made everything a little better. Then I got distracted by this guy in the back. Unremarkable aside from his chunkiness and thick lenses, MD stood against the back wall holding the book between his hands. It was like he was meditating. But he wouldn't stop grinning at me. MD's look of—I don't know, euphoria?—was the furthest thing from a listening face. I remember he seemed so out of place. I was uncomfortable, even lost my place for a second. Then at the signing, he had me inscribe two books: one to MD and another to Holden Caulfield. I thought it was odd, sure. I questioned him with my eyes, but he just kept that inane grin glued on his face.

"Do you really owe it to your brother?" he'd said, pointing to the book. "Is this really him?"

"Sure," I said. "He's here too. Out having a smoke."

His eyes got wide and he nearly pushed people out of his way to get to the door. He almost left his books behind, he was so eager to get out. At the time, I was relieved to be rid of him. But had I known then what I know now...

The Dakota is pretty much deserted. It's the same doorman in the sentry, whom, I'm surprised to note, Alden greets by name. José seems like a nice enough guy, but hardly stacked enough to ward off any real danger. If I were living in a classy place like the Dakota, I would want a bodybuilder for a doorman. A bodybuilder with a machete.

Alden and I kick at the sidewalk a bit. After rushing over here, I feel like we should do *something*. We can't just leave. Maybe we should call the cops. But there's no one here.

Then we hear it.

Psst.

Alden is staring across the street. I follow his gaze to this restaurant, Dakota Grill, which is closed and dark inside. One of the shrubs in front is wiggling like something out of a kids' show. Alden bolts across the street, nearly getting hit by a New York taxi. I follow when there's a lag in traffic.

"MD? What the hell are you doing?" Alden says to the shaking shrub.

MD starts giggling in the bushes. His duffle bag thumps onto the sidewalk. I'm tempted to grab it and run. If he had a weapon, it would be in there, wouldn't it?

He emerges from the shrub, his hair all askew, and I notice a bulge in the right pocket of his trench coat, which appears to be a folded piece of cardboard. I stare at the bulge; that cardboard could be hiding his weapon. Sweat sticks to the back of my neck. Alden's focused on MD's face; I should warn him.

"Well," MD is saying. "I wanted to go back to my hotel, but I just couldn't. I'm waiting for him. Oh, Alden, you missed it! You missed everything."

"Did you get your autograph?" Alden says.

"Did I ever. Look at this." MD holds up his *Double Fantasy* album, which is signed in large, angular pen strokes: *John Lennon December 1980.* "And not only that," MD says, his eyes shining. "I met his son. Little Sean came out to the courtyard with his nanny. I shook his hand."

"Wow," Alden says. "That's awesome. Word."

"So," I say. "Why are you still here? Didn't you get what you came for?"

He stares at the Dakota, which looks much different at night. Spookier, with the spires and turrets and yellowish hue, like it's faded from the sun. There are gargoyles along the iron fence detail. I hadn't noticed that before. A few beats pass in silence. Across the street, José the doorman is reading a newspaper at the sentry. I watch my breath in vapor against the darkness, and hope to God this is it. This calm will be all we see tonight.

MD hands me a brand-new copy of my book. "I bought a new one today," he says to me. "I signed it. Keep it. You'll need it later." He pushes it into my stomach, as if paying off a debt.

Then he starts talking again, and the more he says, the less I understand. Pure nonsense.

"There's a plan for everyone, I believe. God has a plan and the Devil has a plan. And everyone has a two-fold persona within them. It's not God versus Devil per se, but we all have an adult that's trying very hard to be an adult. And we all have a child. A child that never goes away. The Devil tempts the child, but gets real trouble with the adult. God is constant and awe-inspiring. He can save us if we know which way is His. But they each have a plan,

God and the Devil. They have a plan for each of us. It's up to you to decide which is the right one. For me, it's a little of both. They're both instructing me. You have to feel it. And I feel it. I know who's won. That's the big part."

I don't know how Alden feels listening to this rant, but I'm completely freaked out. Alden clears his throat. "What do you mean, MD?" he says. "What's your *plan*?"

"Chapter twenty-seven, Alden! Chapter twenty-seven! We're going to write it," he says, pointing from Alden to the Dakota. "You take that fame and you build your own story. The child and the adult conspire together to kill the phony. And then it's yours. The big part wins. Or you dispose of it, the hypocrisy. For what is fame but air? Some get hooked like it's a narcotic and it messes with their perception of reality. But it *is* just air. That's the thing we are protecting. To the child none of it matters. But the child knows as the Devil has instructed. The adult prays to God…but he's a fake adult, another phony, and it's too late."

I'm shaking. What is this maniacal gibberish? It's not the words he uses as much as his tone. Breathy. High-pitched and sing-songy. His gaze is steady, but at nothing. Every once in a while he rolls his eyes, a twitch.

I'm truly fucking scared. Who knows what this man is capable of? Alden must feel it too; his face is tight with panic.

"MD, listen to me." Alden, my brave brother, grabs MD by the shoulders and gets in his face. "I was a scared, sixteen-year-old boy when I wrote that. My kid brother had just died and I was confused and alone. I didn't know what to do with my anger. I blamed everyone else. I hated the world—and everyone who made the rules in the world…the rules that allowed a little kid to get a terrible disease and die. But, MD, there is no chapter twenty-seven. That book ended. It's final. There isn't a hidden message or part two. Do you hear me?"

MD smiles at him. It's eerie. "MD," I try. "Do you have a weapon?"

"This is not fiction, Alden." He gestures to the book under my arm. "This is reality. Holden Caulfield may not actually empty bullets into another's stomach, although he talks a good game. No, your character is a sensitive fellow. I know this. I empathize, because it's my sensitivity that makes me see clearly what others cannot. Things bother me. Things that other people let roll off their backs." He takes Alden's hands in his own. "But, Alden, this is reality. We can make this real now. We can make this ours."

Alden has turned completely white. He looks like he's going to throw up.

"Tell us what you're planning," I say, hoping my voice reaches him. "MD, we want to help you."

He's misunderstood me. "Are you in too, Alden?"

"MD," Alden says, his voice shaking. "Think about this. You don't want to hurt John Lennon. You waited *all day* for an autograph. I mean—goddam—you were singing *Imagine* at the top of your lungs. You're not a murderer. You're a fan!"

"Thus the hypocrisy. Imagine no possessions? Look where he's living! Alden, it's got to be Lennon. That's the beauty of it. He encapsulates what's wrong with the world today. He's the personification of the decline of human morality. He's irreverent. A heathen. And he has no idea what's about to happen, that cocky bastard."

"No! MD, no. John Lennon is an artist, and his art is the way he communicates. Geez, MD, he's an activist for *peace*. You're missing his whole point! And that one time—for real—he was just making an *analogy* about Jesus and the Beatles. Maybe it was a careless remark, right. But he would never hurt anyone."

"He's already hurt! He's hurt you, he's hurt your brother, and he's hurt me. He hurts society. I can't believe you don't see this. He's it, Alden. He is the ideology that poisons people."

"No, he's just a dude who makes music. He's a man with a wife and a family who happens to make music. End of story."

MD snickers. "They've gotten to you, haven't they? The little people. I told them my mind is made up and I'll tell you the same thing. If you don't want to help, you don't have to, but I have my orders and the decision is done."

Alden shakes his head quickly. "MD! Listen. Did you realize the Beatles use the word 'love' in their songs, like, over six hundred times? Love, MD. Love!" Alden holds his hands in surrender and says, "There's no enemy here."

"Fucking hypocrite!" MD yells, his voice booming down the street.

He reaches into the cardboard bulge in his pocket. I'm frozen in place, watching. Alden lunges and latches onto

MD's elbow, but his grip slips off the trench coat like it's coated with butter.

It's like slow motion: MD retrieves his gun. It's out now. Exposed to the air. I gasp at the sight of it. He's trying to position it, but he fumbles. As he concentrates on inserting his finger into the trigger hole, Alden makes a move. He slaps the gun down, and MD nearly drops it.

MD twists away and repositions his hands. Alden reaches around and yanks on MD's wrist brace.

"Damn you!" MD yells.

The gun drops and MD scurries after it. Alden tries to jump him while he's bent over, but his trench coat is too slick. MD's got the gun again.

It's happening quickly. The downward spiral is like a cyclone, pulling us all into it. I will myself to move. Do something! My breath comes back in bursts. There isn't time—

José the doorman!

I run across the street. "Call the police!" I shout to him.

José is confused. He wants the whole story. I convince him with two words: *gun* and *emergency*. He's on the phone when I see the limousine round the corner onto 72nd Street. I watch MD from across the street; every second seems like a year.

MD's eyes narrow on the limo as it pulls up. I panic. I'm not sure how much time we have. No more than a minute? The limo has stopped.

What should I do? A diversion: I wave my arms and whoop like a primate. But MD's face is set. Alden tries to push him down in a body-lock, but it's like MD's got concrete feet—steady in his orthopedic shoes. As he tries to take aim, Alden tries to get him in a headlock. MD shoves him away, his hand brace slapping Alden's chest with surprising force. Alden breaks his fall, crab-style. While Alden's down, MD steps off the sidewalk and prepares his stance. The gun flashes, reflecting streetlights.

My ears stop working. It's like I'm watching one of my movies with the volume turned low. My pounding heart overrides all other sounds.

At the limo: Yoko is out first. She nods to José, who flutters a frantic hand in warning—but it's lost on her. She pauses at the entrance, turns back to her husband. Lennon angles out of the limo, his hands full of cassette tapes. There's an air of irritation about him. My dinner sits in my throat and I realize MD is right; they have no idea what's about to happen.

Across the street, Alden is scrambling off the ground. MD is out of his reach. He's got his arms outstretched, gun steady. He cocks it and crouches for better aim.

"Mr. Lennon!" he calls.

Now, I think. I have to do something. Now!

"Get down!" I scream, "Gun!" I run toward them with my hands in the air, waving the damn book around. Yoko has turned around, her face contorted with confusion. Lennon turns his gaze, as if in slow motion. I see his signature round glasses, the straight line of his nose. His expression is curious, a little perturbed. No—

"No!" I scream to him. *Go!* I want to say. *Run!* But there is no more time.

I hear it first; it must be three or four shots. I'm thrown, like some incredible force has punched me in the back.

The book goes flying. Was Lennon hit? I can't see anymore. I don't feel anything until my knees hit the concrete, then there's a burning white arc of pain like lightning in my chest. I want to cry out but my breath is gone, my mouth is shocked silent, gaping. My shoulders jolt and I'm on all fours. Everything's blurry. I fall onto my side, dizzy. Am I fainting? I must close my eyes because everything goes black.

There's a woman screaming. I think it's Janine but I know it cannot possibly be.

Chapter 35
Alden

Mom says no one is sick in heaven. No one feels pain. There is no sadness. She prays by my bedside. Most of the time it's a silent prayer. Her eyes closed and lips parted just enough for me to see her tongue tapping her teeth. She thinks it helps me cope: prayer. I don't have the heart to tell her not to bother. It's not that I don't believe. That's not it. I just don't see how it will make a difference. So many people have prayed for me. All my relatives. Friends. Teachers. Nurses. Complete strangers even. But I'm still sick. Maybe it makes her feel better to pray. Maybe it's not about me at all. I like what she told me, though. It's kind of cool to think about not being sick in heaven. That will be a good thing.

Daniel's eyes are closed. Must be asleep. I rub his feet through the blanket a while. Some days they flutter open when I stop reading, but not today. Seems he's gone to sleep. I fold down the page so I know where to pick up tomorrow.

It's been six months since Jerry was killed. Seasons have changed everywhere but here in California. It's now spring, the time of nature's renewal. Rebirth. Change. You don't see a dramatic difference here in Cali, but things do feel different. Everything has since that day. I won't ever be able to demarcate time differently. It will always be in terms of when Jerry died.

After Jerry was gone, I guess you could say I grew up a bit. I stopped smoking chonger. Period. I even cut back on the regular smokes, if you can believe it. I'm also volunteering again. Word, I'm not going to leave it to the Teresas of the world to do good deeds. I can rub a sick person's feet as well as she can, I just needed the courage. Thanks to Jerry, I've got it now.

I decided that I am a decent person—and turns out that's all you need. I made the decision, and as hard as it was, I went back to Daniel's room. His parents and I came up with an arrangement for my visits. While they tend to the chores of real life on Mondays and Wednesdays—calling insurance companies, researching alternative treatments, setting up fund-raisers—I stay with Daniel. It's hard, I can't lie. Daniel's in rough shape. The doctors have all but lost their optimism for his survival, and even I can see he's fading fast. He's happy to see me, though. Every time. And he still has lucid moments. Regrettably, those are the times when he's most scared.

So, at those times, I read to him. I'm reading him *Allie*. I brought my manuscript in after a week or so, thinking it might take his mind off things. After the first chapter, he was hooked. Now he asks for me to read as often as he is able to listen. It felt funny at first, reading my stuff aloud and seeing Daniel's reaction. His eyes wander beneath their lids, and his pale lips turn up when I get to a funny part. Hope he gets to hear the end, 'cause even though it's based on a tragedy, it does have a happy ending. I think he and Allie will hit it off, too.

I've given up trying to publish it. Never heard back from Mitch, nor do I expect to. It's probably still wallowing in his slush. But it doesn't matter. Maybe the whole public forum thing is not for me after all. This seems to be what it's all about anyway. Daniel. *He's* why I wrote it. I'm helping him. *Allie* is sending him out of this world with a smile on his face, and something close to hope in his heart. That's enough audience for me. More than enough.

Fiona and big Dave had their baby girl. Marie Elizabeth, they named her, after our mother. She's a cutie. Chubby as a pumpkin. Bald as a cue ball, but I'll bet she's got hair like her momma's coming in soon. Kiki and I went back just after she was born and stayed with them for a long weekend. Turns out, Kiki is a natural with babies.

Kiki and I live together in Jerry's place. We're best friends first, lovers second. Maybe one day we'll get hitched, but we're not in any rush. We kinda fell into it after what happened to Jerry. Kind of held onto each other, a grasp at peace.

I remember it like it just happened. Geez, it was so fast. Struggling with MD for his gun, the surprising strength of his arms, how impossibly slippery his goddam trench coat was. If I hadn't been pushed to the ground, would it have turned out differently? Because by the time I got up, he'd already pulled the trigger four times. As I wrestled him to the ground, a fifth shot was sent into the air. They say it comes back down at the same speed, but— whatever—I couldn't worry about that.

The fuzz were there by then, and got MD in handcuffs in two seconds flat. They didn't even ask me any questions. Didn't have to. MD was out of his mind talking static about completing his mission and how the Devil knows and will find a way, and all that garbage. He gave them a copy of the book saying it was his statement. His big promotional stunt. How freaking lame. Unreal.

John and Yoko were hurried into the safety of their apartment building. By the time they had MD in the police car, I was across the street at the entrance of the Dakota, cradling my brother's head in my lap, stroking his hair, telling him he'd be okay. I didn't know where he'd been shot. Just knew he was down.

When I saw all the blood pooling around us, I knew it was bad. The ambulance was there and the paramedics were doing their thing. They ripped open his clothes and I saw the worst, goriest scene of my life. But I wouldn't leave him. No one told me I had to move, so I stayed with him, tried to ignore my own shock and talk to him, my voice cracking from tears. As they were snapping the stretcher in place, Jerry held onto my hand really hard. He looked up at me, his eyes out of focus, and said, "Are they safe?"

I told him they were. Told him not to worry. He tried to say something else, but I couldn't make it out. I hunched down, got my ear right near his lips.

"I'm so sorry," he said.

I lost it. Started bawling like a goddam little kid. I told him over and over it wasn't his fault, but he couldn't hear me. He couldn't hear anything. His eyes went glassy, his breathing got patchy. He died in the ambulance on the way to the hospital. I stayed with him all night, though. Just couldn't break myself away.

I waited until morning to call Fiona. She took it pretty rough. Felt like it was her fault. As much as I told her it wasn't, she couldn't stop blaming herself. She was getting herself so worked up, big Dave started to worry about the baby. She eventually went to see a counselor who gave her something to help her sleep.

Baby Marie has certainly given her something to smile about, though. That's the good thing. It will be a long process for all of us, but life goes on.

It's a little awkward living in Jerry's old place. Kiki and I talked about moving, getting away from it all. Going to Colorado or someplace where the air is totally fresh and nature can take your mind to different places. But we decided that we weren't done in LA. Kiki had just started her job before our god-awful trip to New York. And I had some unfinished business too. In the name of Daniel Halsted.

People sometimes ask me if I'm still writing. I am. But it's not what they think. My next project is to lobby Congress for some serious gun control. Look what's happened, just because a lunatic was able to procure a weapon and exercise his useless, careless will. I can't even think about it, it ticks me off so bad. MD's trial is going on right now and even though I refuse to acknowledge the SOB, I've heard that he's reading the book in the courtroom. Not even paying attention to the judge. Waves it to the paparazzi whenever they're near. Makes me want to take the book out of print, I swear to

God. I don't think I even knew what it meant to be a pacifist, until now.

I remember all those times I used to toss up that silent prayer to Allie: *Don't let me disappear...* As if my baby brother were my anchor to this earth. As if his death had opened the heavens, which could then reach down with cloudy mitts to grasp me and bring me to an eternal, misty fog of grief. I was sure I'd be that scared little kid for the rest of my life. But it's all different now. Mom's gone. Jerry's gone. Perhaps Daniel will be too. I'm not saying it doesn't suck. But I think I can at least keep my own feet on the ground, and find a way to conceive of a future—even if they aren't in it. But I know it's not my time to disappear. And I can't be scared of tomorrow. That doesn't do anybody any favors. Especially me.

Every evening, Kiki and I watch the sun set through Jerry's bay window—painting splendor in broad, warm strokes over the litter and smoke stacks. I love this lame view now. I don't know if I could ever leave. How many sunsets are enough in a lifetime? Did Jerry see enough? It kills me, he got so gypped. I told him I loved him before the light went out of his eyes. I hope to God he heard me.

Author's Word & Acknowledgments

Years ago as a student teacher at Andover High School, my mentor handed me a VHS tape of an old Dateline video that featured Mark David Chapman's fixation on *The Catcher in the Rye* and its influence in his murder of John Lennon. Every subsequent year I taught *Catcher*, I would play that video for my class—and found myself equal parts enthralled and horrified with the tragedy again and again.

This book was born from that fascination of mine—how a novel could move someone to act in such an extreme way. I also couldn't help but wonder what Holden would have thought if he knew what his words triggered. One of my writing teachers once said it is sometimes easier to outline your novel from the "crisis" backward. In order to place Alden (Holden) where Lennon was shot, I had to publish the report he wrote in the mental clinic (his journal aka *The Catcher in the Rye*) and somehow have him meet Mark David Chapman. As the book evolved, it no longer became about this incident, but how three siblings had to overcome serious familial issues. Each character is my invention alone, an artistic expression inspired by *Catcher* characters Holden, DB, and Phoebe. This book is in no way based on the life of JD Salinger, nor is it a statement about JD Salinger as a person or an author. And so, first and foremost, with utmost respect: Thank you, Mr. Salinger, for writing *The Catcher in the Rye*.

The 2013 *Amazon Breakthrough Novel Award* contest validated my concept after dozens (dozens!) of rejections. Thanks to all my "fans" who read my excerpt, gave me a five-star rating, and wanted to read more. Your votes of encouragement gave me that final push to perfect my manuscript and get it out into the world.

I'm forever grateful for my tenure at Newburyport High School and the opportunity to work with Susie Galvin and the best English department on the planet.

Steve Alcorn and *The Writing Academy* provided me the tools to polish my final product.

Jenna Blum's *Stormchasers* beautifully portrayed a sister who is desperate to take care of her troubled brother, helping to shape my sibling characters and their complex relationships.

Deborah Daw Heffernan, after reading three chapters, warned me of the difficulties in establishing a single believable voice, no less three. How right she was.

My early readers—Erika Grahl Cogliani and the entire Caballero family—loved the book before it was any good.

Thank you, Cassandra Dunn, for the extraordinary manuscript critiques.

Tember Fasulo (and her four new "friends") at Amazon provided the high res ABNA star image for the cover design.

David Corbett (*The Art of Character*) encouraged me to get into the skin of Mark David Chapman, teaching me that the best writing comes from our most uncomfortable or vulnerable places.

My writing life would be very lonely without my talented writer friends: Anika Denise, Alyson Aiello, Michelle Curran, Kelly Van Hull, Sandra Hume. Your insight and general cheerleading for the written word have been an enormous support. Anika's PR expertise helped this book in more ways than one.

Sandra Hume is probably the most valuable reader and editor one could have. I was so relieved that you liked my first draft. (winJerryreaker, hanJerryag...LOL!) Thank you for your invaluable overall edits, your rock-star copy editing skills, your constant words of encouragement, and your cherished friendship. This book would not be the same without you.

Thanks to my in-laws—Judith & Sam Basile, and Robin & Mike Spero—for your love and support, always. Judith, I can always trust your discerning opinion on various works of literature, including mine. I love crashing your book club, and I look forward to your next book recommendation, as it never disappoints.

My talented brother, Jimmy, encourages me to think about structure when all I want to do is write with my head in the clouds. Thanks for all the talks, the brainstorming, the noodling out of plot problems. Thank you for sharing your remarkable brain. My sis-in-law, Vanessa, sent me the sweetest note of encouragement when I needed it most.

Descendants of talented wordsmiths, my parents gave me the best gift: writing talent. Janet and Jim Davies, thank you for reading multiple drafts, for your enthusiasm, endless support, and unconditional love. Mom, you not only inspired me to change careers and teach, but you helped brainstorm the concept for this very novel on the way to DFW airport. Remember?

My boy collection, AJ, Adam, and Chaz, inspires me every day to be a good mom and a better person.

Last but not least, thanks to my loving husband, Anthony Joseph Spero—the best person I know and my model for altruism. Anthony, none of this is possible without you; you are behind everything I do, every thought I have, and every word I write.

Catcher's Keeper

Bibliography

Chapters where the following works have been either quoted or paraphrased are noted below.

Fawcett, Anthony. *John Lennon, One Day at a Time.* New York, NY. Grove Press, 1976. Print.

Jones, Jack. *Let Me Take You Down: Inside the Mind of Mark David Chapman, the Man Who Killed John Lennon.* New York, NY. Villard Books, 1992. Print. *Chapters 28, 32, 34*

Keats, John. "Ode On A Grecian Urn." Poetry X. Ed. Jough Dempsey. 16 Jun 2003. 04 Aug. 2013 <http://poetry.poetryx.com/poems/326/>.

Salinger, J.D. *The Catcher in the Rye.* New York, NY. Little, Brown and Company, 1951. Print. *Quoted in italics in chapters: 1, 2, 24, 28, 29, 32*

Discussion Questions

1. Between 1961 and 1982, *The Catcher in the Rye* was the most censored book in high schools and libraries in the United States, although those opposed to the novel were often unfamiliar with the plot itself. Reasons for censorship included: vulgarity, sexual references, blasphemy, lack of morality and familial values, and promotion of rebellion, alcoholic consumption, smoking, lying, and promiscuity.

In Chapter 24, Jerry is interviewed by a newspaper reporter (Heffernan) and addresses some of the controversy mentioned above in the novel. If you are familiar with *The Catcher in the Rye*, how would you answer Heffernan's questions as a reader? Put yourself in Salinger's shoes: How would you answer Heffernan's questions as an author?

2. Other gunmen besides Mark David Chapman have credited *The Catcher in the Rye* for their acts of violence: Robert John Bardo's murder of Rebecca Schaeffer and John Hinckley, Jr.'s assassination attempt on Ronald Reagan. Considering this, do you agree that *The Catcher in the Rye* should have been banned? Should it be banned today?

3. Alden, at forty, is still reluctant to join the world of grown-ups. What are some examples of his immaturity? By the end of the novel, in what ways does he mature?

4. What would you do if your sibling stole your teenage journal and published it without your permission?

5. Daniel Halsted and Alden's brother, Allie, both suffer(ed) from a terrible disease. How does childhood disease/death shape Alden's character? How does it shape Jerry's character?

6. How is Fiona's desire to become a mother symbolic of her relationship with her brothers?

7. Despite what it might do to save his struggling career, what are the real reasons Jerry stole Alden's journal? Why did he agree to publish it? Or, do you believe he always meant to publish it?

8. Hubris is commonly defined in classic literature as "extreme arrogance that leads to a character's downfall." How is hubris shown in this novel?

9. How does Kiki's relationship with her sister affect Alden's relationship with Jerry?

10. Teresa is both Alden's and Fiona's lost love. How do her actions shape Alden's and Fiona's choices? How do you reconcile Teresa's contradicting character traits (altruist and heartbreaker)?

11. Fiona's mistake in telling MD about Jerry's theft is a turning point in the novel and for Fiona's character. What

do we learn about Fiona in this interaction with MD and its ramifications?

12. Jerry's character starts to change when he embarks on the book tour. Do you feel Jerry finds redemption by the end of the novel?

13. If you were introduced to MD as Alden was, would you also believe him to be "harmless"? Or, did Alden miss some obvious red flags?

14. Do you think the characters had a moral responsibility to try to stop MD?

15. The real Mark David Chapman has received "fan mail" from other convicted murderers, congratulating him on killing a celebrity rather than an ordinary civilian, to which Chapman has publicly expressed disgust. He has been known to regret killing John Lennon. Do you think the MD that appears in this novel would regret killing Jerry?

16. One could say Alden's life has been shaped by his grief in losing his baby brother, Allie. How do you think his life will be affected by losing his older brother, Jerry?

17. Alden's journal (aka *The Catcher in the Rye*) could be seen as a character (the antagonist) in this novel. How does Alden manage to overcome the conflict it represents?

18. *Publisher's Weekly* reviewed an earlier version of this novel and had this to say about it and *The Catcher in the Rye*:

Imagine if Holden Caulfield were a real person, 40 years old in 1980. Imagine if The Catcher in the Rye *were written by this Holden as his high school journal, and when his older brother reads it, he publishes it as his own under the pen name JD Gallagher. The journal comes to the attention of MD who will use it as an inspiration to kill celebrities, such as John Lennon. But MD and Holden meet. This* Catcher in the Rye *"sequel" has Holden (now named Alden) speaking in an amalgam of his original slang ("crumby" and "phony") with some more 1980s slang ("grody" and "Word!"). For those who found Holden a whiny immature brat in the original, imagine how he comes across with essentially the same personality as a middle-aged man. A subplot with sister "Fiona" attempting to get pregnant adds nothing to the story. It's hard to imagine who would hate this more— those who loved the original* The Catcher in the Rye, *or those who hated it.*

How do you feel about the author's style of Alden's voice? Is it believable? Do you agree that Fiona's attempt to get pregnant "adds nothing to the story"? Did you hate *The Catcher in the Rye* or did you love it?

Made in the USA
Charleston, SC
01 December 2015